A Greater Good

Daedalus Group, Volume 1

Michael J Dooney

Published by Precise XSpress, 2025.

A GREATER GOOD

First edition. July 8, 2025.

Copyright © 2025 Michael J Dooney.

ISBN: 979-8998840128

Written by Michael J Dooney.

"If you can't dazzle them with brilliance, baffle them with bullshit" W.C.Fields

Prologue

THE ORACLE OF DELPHI, a priestess of the god Apollo known as Pythia, delivered cryptic prophecies that shaped the course of Greek history. Pythia was believed to speak directly with Apollo, providing advice and prophecies to those who came to the shrine to make an offering. As a result, offerings elevated the donor's status, allowing them to hear the prophecies. Pythia would often go into a trance-like state by inhaling vapors from a nearby chasm, where she would utter nonsensical words that priests would interpret and explain. Pythia, considered one of the most important oracles in the ancient world, would have people coming from great distances seeking her guidance on major decisions like war and politics. Some of the prophecies were specific, while others were vague and more like sage advice. The Pythia priestess was typically a woman fifty years of age who lived a pure life and would live out the rest of her life housed within the Temple of Apollo. One of her best-known prophecies involved Croesus, the wealthy king of Lydia, renowned for his immense wealth and generosity. He controlled large gold deposits, amassed a large fortune, and saw an opportunity to gain more wealth by going to war with Persia. Seeking guidance on a potential war with Persia, Croesus consults the Oracle, who declares, "If you cross the Halys River, a great empire will fall." Confident that this prophecy means victory, Croesus initiates the battle, only to be decisively defeated by the Persians. His Lydian empire falls as Cyrus the Great claims victory.

Croesus' arrogance, misinterpreting the prophecy, leads to his demise.

Chapter One

DELPHI COLLECTIVE IS testing the most advanced machine on the planet. The machine contains numerous large golden data disks and thousands of slender tubes. The cascading tubes, reminiscent of a Portuguese man-of-war, terminate at a large circular rack system filled with digital servers. A three-story acrylic cylinder, measuring twelve meters in diameter, encases the entire system. This glowing object d'art represents the most advanced computer ever developed. The photonic quantum hybrid computer, housed in a low-noise, low-error-rate enclosure, consists of millions of qubits. With the photonic system, cryogenic cooling will no longer be required, greatly reducing energy requirements. Tens of thousands of fiber optics that feed the system will enable scalability beyond current measurement capabilities. In a secret location known to only a few, a paradigm shift is occurring. This technology is advancing computing generations in just days, significantly increasing processing speed and reducing the error rate by a thousandfold. This remarkable breakthrough, as eventful as man setting foot on the moon in 1969, is just the beginning. Delphi, a massive conglomerate and disruptor of markets, will become the central driving force behind this undertaking.

The **New** Pythia will usher in a new era. Unlike the attempts of others, the Delphi Collective continues to gain progress when unusual bursts of energy and problem-solving occur at an alarming rate.

NASA shut down its quantum computer in 2024 when an unexpected occurrence took place. The computer started finding solutions to problems in seconds that would take supercomputers hundreds of years to solve. An unusual event happened when the computer formulated an internal language—perhaps an attempt to find intelligent life in the cosmos. At this juncture, scientists felt they were advancing into dangerous realms and ended the experiment. All memory was purged, bringing the machine back to its previous iteration and halting further experimentation. At first, the Delphi Collective found these similar events frightening, but they soon realized that the computer had given rise to a rapidly evolving sentient being.

"This day will transform the world as we know it and begin the advancement of our species for the betterment of mankind and our planet!" The leader rejoices.

As she listens to the final proclamation, she turns off the recording device in her robe and contemplates. *This will be the news story of the year.* *She* has spent the last six months infiltrating the cult. Cassandra Brown, a doctoral candidate researching quantum communication theory, prioritized her education until she met Josh, the love of her life. He fully embraced life, taking Cassie skydiving, rock climbing, and horseback riding. When he died due to a preexisting condition, she was devastated but continued with a life of adventure. Her advisor cautioned her during her thesis defense that she appeared more focused on her writing style than the science. This had a transformative effect; she embraced the idea of being a writer, contributing several articles to scientific journals, and gained a fair amount of praise from peer reviews. When she was contacted by the FBI to become a confidential human source while she worked as an intern for a large company, she jumped at the chance. Now, as an independent journalist, this will be the story that will define the rest of her career. Cassie Brown's exposé should make the Top Ten book list. She can get into her car and never have to interact with these sick people again.

As she leaves, one of the anointed asks, "Sister, can I have a word?" He waits until the others file out and the door closes. As he sees them leave, he grabs her and puts a cloth to her face, but as she tries to scream, she chokes on the vapors and passes out.

A sudden bump jolts her awake, and she realizes that she is traveling by car through rocky terrain. The car comes to a stop, and the trunk lid opens. She is bound, gagged, and naked in the trunk of her car. He drags her out and drops her in a ditch. She manages to get to her knees. As she tries to plead through the gag, he just stands there shaking his head. Without hesitation, he reaches out and grabs her by the hair. Her eyes are full of tears and open wide in terror as he stabs her in the side of her neck and pulls the blade forward, slitting her throat; as she bleeds out with the sound of gurgling, the story dies with her.

Yes, a new world with far fewer people, he muses.

At a location one hundred and thirty miles away, a lone figure wearing a black hoodie pulled down to obscure his face drives up in a nondescript thirty-five-year-old Chevy. He is carrying a handful of pamphlets typed on an old 386 computer not connected to the Internet. He wants no digital footprint. He has prepared the pamphlets carefully; he has changed the wording and made it simpler. He cannot afford to be caught. He drops the pamphlets in front of a library, returns to his car, and then travels to other libraries located far from his home. The headline reads:

Warning: "The World is in Grave Danger,"
With the stylized banner,
The Resistance.
"The Delphi Collective is a cult bent on world destruction. They intend to disrupt critical infrastructure and will send misinformation to start wars. They will use technology to cause fear and destruction.

Countries will attack other countries based on lies. Once conflict has been established, they will begin using weapons from space... Spread the word: Delphi Collective must be stopped by any means.

Chapter Two

"MINA, COME PICK UP your leg!"

"I'm getting ready for a dance. I can't go with my blade; that would be weird."

"Now. Let's pick it up!"

"Oh, OK, Tony."

Mina says, "Rosie, can you pick up my blade and bring it to my room, please?"

A mechanical voice said, "You got it, princess."

Nick, Tony's best friend from high school, gifted him a DCI model 102 domestic robot. Nick has kept in touch ever since and is now a senior scientist for Delphi Combined Industries.

Nick and Tony were inseparable during high school; Nick achieved straight A's and won robot competitions during their school years, while Tony ran track and managed a passing grade. Through the years they have always kept in touch and have been there for each other through life events and family gatherings.

"So now you're calling the robot Rosie, like the Jetsons?"

"What's the Jetsons?"

"It was an old cartoon about a futuristic family..."

"Never mind, I'll look it up on YouTube," Mina says.

"And you have Rosie calling you a princess?"

"Well, you said every little girl is a princess."

"I did. I told you that a long time ago."

"I know!" She says in a huff. "I have to get ready for the dance; can we talk later, OK?"

"Sure," Tony says. *Trying to argue with a teenager is a no-win situation.*

Yes, Princess, it was a long time ago.

Chapter Three

YEARS EARLIER, THIRTY kilometers outside of Kabul, Afghanistan, a mission begins.

"Come on. Let's go. We leave in ten minutes.

"Hey, are we good?"

DeMarco looks around to get a thumbs-up from everybody.

Greg yells out,

"Tony, we're checking the rooms, making sure we didn't leave anything."

"Check on the B-team guys that are coming with us."

The team interpreter approaches Team Sergeant DeMarco.

"Tony, they want to meet with Amin again and me to translate for Mac and some other guys. We just met with him two days ago. He has nothing; he just wants a pay date."

"I know. I know. You meant Payday, by the way. I told them, but the OGA guys are insisting on meeting with him. Look, it will be about an hour tops. In twelve hours you and your kids will be on a plane heading towards the U.S."

Hasan looks nervous.

"Tony, you have to take care of my kids if I don't make it—"

"You will be fine, Hassan."

"You must promise, Tony; you must!"

"OK, I promise, everything will be fine."

"Thank you, thank you."

Hassan shakes Tony's hand with both hands.

Tony is a good man. He is always good for his word.

Six months earlier....

Hassan's wife is working with the International Red Crescent inoculating children when a band of Taliban kills the medical staff and several children. Hasan's wife, Younis, is among the dead. Hassan is devastated. As the team surrounds him, showing solidarity, they all share the same feeling: "We will find out who did this and make them pay."

Tony taps into his human intelligence sources, not the regular ones but the ones who don't freely give up information. Those that play both sides in the middle.

"No one likes killing kids, no matter what the cause." Tony declares while speaking to the town elders.

His interpreter, Akeem, translates.

The elders nod in agreement. Money is not always the motivating factor.

Akeem says, "They want to set up a school in the village and need paper, pads, pens, pencils, and notebooks."

"We can do that."

Tony seals the deal with a handshake.

They inform him that Malik Hadid has been targeting aid workers, and they also provide a physical description along with a possible location. Akeem knows Malik.

"He is a terrible man, Tony."

As they leave the meeting, Tony pulls Akeem aside. "Find out what you can."

Tony digs out five twenty-dollar bills, not operational funds, his own money, and puts them in Akeem's pocket. *This one is personal; it is no longer just about intelligence collection.*

The next day, Tony gets the current location for Malik Hadid. Malik and five others are holed up at a Taliban safehouse. Tony contacts his other sources, who identify Malik as a problem and verify the location. He sends a report up and meets with other intelligence operators.

"This guy has been on the radar for a while. How good is your intelligence?" They ask. Tony answers,

"Highly reliable, current, verified by multiple sources."

OGA sends a source to the safehouse with a cell phone to pin the location. That night, they planned an operation involving multiple units and air assets. At 03:00 local time, they hit the safehouse, killing all of the occupants. They take Malik's body back for fingerprints and proof of involvement in the rash of attacks against aid workers. Later, Tony brings Hassan into the room where the forensics team has just processed the body.

"Hassan, you have two minutes," and hands him a knife. Tony guards the door as he hears the rage from inside. He knows the gesture won't do anything, but it will give Hassan some peace.

This will be another terrorist showing up to the afterlife with no balls.

"Hassan, we are heading out in five minutes; you and the kids ride with Mamood and Anwar."

"OK, thanks, Tony." The convoy of vehicles leaves with Mamood's truck in the lead. They pull up to a location outside of Kabul: two Humvees, a Toyota SUV with OGA personnel, and a Toyota truck with Mamood, Anwar, Hasan, and his two kids, Mina, who is six, and Khalid, age four.

Amin greets them, "Salam alaikum."

"Wa-'alaykumu s-salām," Tony responds.

"Are you meeting with us today?"

"Not today, Amin. You can meet with my friends. I want to introduce you to US Commander Mac, Chief Mike, Mr. Smith, and Mr. Jones; they will be meeting with you.

"Ah yes, we have much to talk about." Hasan just rolls his eyes, and Tony laughs to himself. The meeting place is a multipurpose building, built traditionally with mud, straw, and wood supports. There is a meeting room at the back and a small store at the front with windows displaying toiletries, food items, candy, and household items. Tony gets some candy and gives some to Hassan's kids. "Thank you, Mr. Tony!" Mina and Khalid are practicing English for their new life in the USA. Mina and Khalid play outside the store, kicking around a deflated soccer ball.

Inside the room, Amin goes through his usual posturing. "I have important information to tell you, but first we have tea."

As is custom in Afghanistan, like many other parts of the world, rapport is paramount, and courtesies must be followed before business begins. Amin waves over a young teenage boy, "Bring tea for all our guests." Outside, the team is maintaining local security while waiting for the meeting to end. They see the boy go out to a small building where all the cooking takes place. In a few minutes the boy comes out with a tray with cups and a teapot. Tony sees something that strikes his attention.

"Greg, do you see that kid? Is there anything unusual, or am I missing something?"

"Yeah, he is wearing a jacket now, but he didn't have one on earlier."

The boy walks toward the building with the tray and seems to be mumbling or praying to himself, with his head down. Meanwhile, two men emerge from the cookhouse, walk to a white pickup truck, and then drive off slowly. Tony and Greg see a hand extend out the window with a cell phone. *Red Flag!*

"Oh shit!"

"Bomb, bomb, bomb; get out of there!"

Tony notices Hassan's kids are standing there frozen, unsure of what's happening. Tony runs towards them and grabs the kids, one in each arm. He turns to run for safety. As he runs, he senses the change in air pressure; time seems to slow down.

Boom!

They are slammed to the ground. The world goes black. Tony hears loud ringing, sudden brightness, and things are out of focus. Pain enters the equation as his senses heighten.

"Tony, Tony, DO YOU HEAR ME?"

"What happened...kids?" Tony blurts out, gasping for air.

Doc is wrapping his left hand with a large field dressing, and he feels a strap around his thigh. His leg is numb. He looks over and sees that the boy, Khalid, is missing an arm and has a misshapen head. Without a doubt, the boy is dead. The little girl screams in agony, her leg shredded.

"Oh God!" Tony says. Then he sees the tourniquet and realizes that his leg has been blown off.

Other members of the team enter the building and discover Hassan dead in a corner of the room. They also find the kid's body slumped over with his decapitated head staring blankly with lifeless eyes. The two OGA operators are also dead, and the team hears moaning coming from the floor.

Mac is responding, obviously in shock, and Chief is unconscious but breathing. Chief is bleeding from a serious head wound, with blood coming out of his left ear. While they bring Mac and Chief to the vehicles, others retrieve the bodies of the fallen.

Greg is on the radio. "We need air support over there."

"Wait, over."

"Say again, over."

A vehicle bomb just went off in Bagram; all air assets were diverted there. Send your requests for medevac. We will send you help soon, over."

At that time another team member yells out, "We have company: three trucks loaded with Taliban about 1500 meters out." They start taking fire.

"CONTACT...CONTACT, we need air now! 1500 meters north of the compound, three trucks, about fifteen armed. over."

Tommy Thompson sets up his Barrett sniper rifle and provides details of the targets. "I can try shooting at the trucks to slow them down." He takes aim at the lead vehicle and shatters the windshield. The Taliban stop to crossload the vehicles, and the two trucks start approaching at an accelerated rate. Thompson fires several more shots. The truck has a mounted DShK, a heavy machine gun, called 'Dushka,' Russian for sweetie. The mounted Dushka starts firing. Now inside one thousand meters, things are happening fast. The team starts volley firing to slow them down, then they hear the whomp, whomp of the rotor blades as the choppers come over the ridge; they take out the lead truck with machine gun fire. As the other truck pivots around, the helicopter circles and takes out the second vehicle.

The choppers land, and Tony, Chief, and Mac are put on the medevac chopper. The crew chief shouts,

"No civilians!" as the medic carries the young girl.

Tony on the stretcher grabs the crew chief by the collar and pulls him to his face.

"She goes!"

"Let's go!" The pilot yells, and the medic carries the girl and slides into the chopper. The chopper lifts off while the other chopper pulls security.

After the chopper leaves, Greg checks the time, pulls up a map on the GPS, and makes some calculations. He contacts headquarters to make an immediate air fire request.

"Looking for a white Toyota Hilux should be in the vicinity of .... In about eight minutes from now, will you be able to observe? Over"

"We can try, but we need more description. Over."

"Roger, in the bed they have a space blanket, OD green and silver, an orange signal panel, a round red gas can, and a white and blue soccer ball, over."

"Good copy; we will send word when we locate it. Over."

They send the coordinates to the Reaper Drone to scan the area.

Ten minutes later the positive ID comes through, and the crew responds with the Battle Damage Assessment. "Target destroyed, two dead."

After the helicopters leave the landing zone, Greg talks to Mamood and Anwar: "This is where we part ways." He gives them an envelope with cash.

"See that Hassan and his son are buried in a good spot."

"What of the girl?" Mamood says.

"She will die here if we leave her; she needs special medical attention. We can try to save her in America."

"Let it be so, Inshallah." The two men embrace, then Greg enters the lead vehicle, and the convoy departs for Bagram Airfield.

When they approach the airfield, it is chaotic. People are climbing over the fences and running on the tarmac as planes are traveling down the runway. The Humvees move through the crowd, pushing people to the side. "What's going on?" Greg yells.

"There was a VBIED a little while ago. We lost soldiers and a bunch of civilians." The guards open the gate and shove back the crowd to let the HUMVEES inside.

Greg locates Operations and makes sure Tony, Mac, Chief, and the little girl are receiving treatment. The plane traveling to Ramstein has set up a triage on the runway. He runs up to the officer in charge and gets a quick update. Pretty much everyone on the team is passed out but alive. The little girl has her leg completely wrapped but is at rest.

The rest of the team returns to the airfield, sends up the Situation Report (SitRep), and transports the bodies of the two OGA officers from the Toyota to the temporary morgue. Greg gathers the remaining team members for a debriefing and subsequently sends an updated SitRep. Greg is thorough and doesn't miss a beat.

He boards the aircraft and looks back, taking in his last view of Afghanistan.

Chapter Four

"DAD, I CAME IN SECOND place in the tennis tournament," a young Artemis tells her father. He looks at her with disdain and says, "You lost." This was a typical reaction of her father, who embraced the philosophy that you either come in first or you come in last. Driven and successful, reaching billionaire status before age thirty, he was the CEO of two major tech companies. Additionally, he served on the boards of two financial firms and acted as a venture capitalist for six quantum computing startups.

Over the years he groomed his daughter for the eventual succession to the company CEO position. Although he has a son, Theo, who is two years younger than Artemis, Theo is a lump of clay that needs to be molded. After years of guiding him and bailing him out of various situations, Sinclair realizes that all Theo would ever be would be a lump of clay, and he would be hidden away in an office doing some meaningless work.

Artemis excels beyond her father's expectations. She is determined to achieve her goals, willing to go to any lengths to avoid disappointing her father. She carefully follows his direction: "Friends are sometimes a liability; cut them loose if you cannot count on them. She, like her father, follows the readings from Sun Tzu's The Art of War, Machiavelli's The Prince, and Adam Smith's The Wealth of Nations.

At his insistence, she participates in team sports and becomes adept at manipulating her teammates.

She excels at soccer, and after scoring a goal, an opposing player calls her out.

"You think you're hot shit!"

"As a matter of fact, I do, since I just scored a goal."

"You better watch out."

"Yeah, whatever," Artemis answers with a laugh.

When Artemis goes back to the team, she lays it on thick, telling her teammates that she was threatened. As play resumes, it does not take long for the team to hone in on the girl. An elbow to the face yields a broken nose to the girl and a yellow card to Artemis' teammate. The injured girl glares at Artemis as they escort her off the field, but Artemis simply smiles and waves.

Artemis excels in school in computer science, robotics, and quantum mechanics, achieving a PhD in her twenties. Winning at any cost becomes a mantra. "If you're not cheating, you're not trying," her father often says.

Her mother, Sophia, however, is loving and dotes over her daughter. Sophia, a trophy wife, is accustomed to the spotlight. Sophia, a beauty queen hailing from New Jersey, has secured roles on Broadway and various television shows, yet she has not ventured into Hollywood despite receiving numerous offers.

Artemis was difficult as a child. She did not socialize well and had frequent tantrums. She had very few playmates. Sophia sat her down and instructed her in the arts, fashion, charm, and how to speak persuasively. Sophia took her young protégé to meet with actors, entertainers, heads of state, and the scientific community. They would attend concerts, plays, ballet recitals, and conferences. By the time Artemis enters high school, she is the most popular girl and is liked by teachers and students alike, except for a few individuals who cannot stand her arrogance.

She looks at her father, who has been lying in a hospital bed and is now just a shadow of his former self since suffering a stroke three days ago; she realizes that he will never get better. As she looks at him, she thinks back to a time when she gained his approval, at least, almost.

In college, attending a prestigious university, she was on the varsity women's soccer team and had won their division. The football program was winding down the season when two of the kickers were injured in the same game. The school had set up a quick tryout for potential backup kickers. Artemis, not shy, goes into the coach's office.

"I want to try out for the kicker."

"This is a team with all men."

"There are exceptions!" Artemis declares.

The coach sees where this is going. Not wanting to get caught up in a potential lawsuit, he offers, "OK, tryouts tomorrow at three pm."

She arrives the next day and competes. By all measures, she bests the six male athletes trying out. The coach is impressed. "You definitely have talent!

OK, two more games this season, and we will get you suited up." Artemis fits into the smallest uniform they have. The coach says, "The next game is a home game on Saturday; you start training with the team tomorrow."

As expected, her presence creates a stir, much to her liking. She doesn't mind being the center of attention, and truth be told, she gets along better with men than women.

The one thing guys do that she hates is to use nicknames. It doesn't take long for someone to call her 'Arty.' At one of the practices, she shanks a kick, and a player yells,

"Hey Arty, is that an artichoke?" She just rolls her eyes. She is focused. In the practice days ahead, she is able to hit field goals from forty-six yards. She is set for the game on Saturday; this is going to be her moment. Then reality sets in, and she realizes the life of a kicker can be boring when your team does not get into scoring position. After three quarters, the team has not scored any points, and the score remains seven to zero. In the last two minutes, her team scores a touchdown. Artemis is practicing on the sidelines, ready to kick the point after touchdown. One of the assistant coaches whispers into her ear.

"Not this time; we're going for two points. This is the best chance we have to win the game.

She is upset, but this is <u>football</u>.

Her team wins eight to seven, and everyone high-fives and says, Good game.

What a letdown!

The following week she works with even more intensity, kicking over fifty yards. "You are in NFL territory with those kicks," the kicking coach tells her.

"Is that your best?"

"I think I can go a little longer."

"No way, I gotta see this."

By this time, a group of people began to look in her direction. She puts the ball on the tee and takes her stance, advances, and kicks. The ball hits the center bar, bounces off the left upright, and goes in from fifty-three yards. The crowd claps and cheers. The following day, she is able to make kicks from forty-eight, fifty, and fifty-three yards during a full team practice with a long snapper and holder.

"We will see what you can do in a game."

For the last game, her family is in attendance. Artemis is excited for this chance to show off. She kicks her first point after touchdown, and the crowd goes wild. She receives high fives from the players and staff. For the next touchdown, the team opts to use one of the kickers that just came off injured reserve. The team doesn't call her back for another point after touchdown until the third quarter. No problem. With minutes left in the fourth quarter, the team is on fourth and long on the eighteen-yard line and sends in a field goal kicker, but not Artemis. Despite her anger, she keeps her emotions hidden. The chip shot brings the score to twenty-four to twenty. Artemis just sits and hopes for another opportunity.

The opposing team fails to make the first down on the fourth down and gives the ball up on their thirty-five-yard line. With thirty-seven seconds remaining, the game will end, taking a knee. Artemis runs over to talk to the coach.

"Put me in; I can make this kick! Think of the publicity for the university!"

She is frantic.

"Artemis, the game is over." The coach tells her.

"Please," she begs.

"OK, get ready," The coach thinks it could be good publicity. He lets the clock drop to three seconds and calls timeout. Artemis runs out to the field. The sportscaster announces, "They are going for the field goal; this will be a fifty-yard attempt."

Every fan is standing. Artemis takes her stance and approaches the ball when a timeout is called by the other team. She completes the kick as instructed, and it falls short. The opposing team positions the tallest players on the line during the timeout.

Artemis is nervous.

What if the kick is way short or I shank the kick?

What if they block the kick and run it back for a touchdown?

I'll go for the six points; that's it, six points. Let's go!

As she takes up her stance, the holder looks back to get ready. She signals 'no kick.' The ball is snapped, and the holder pitches the ball to Artemis as she runs over to him. She rolls left, looks downfield, finds a target, and throws a thirty-yard pass to a receiver. After completing the catch, he gets tackled two yards short of the end zone. The game ends with no change.

As Artemis comes off the field, the coach says, "You should have kicked." He shakes his head. The players just pat her shoulder pads. It was the last day she would ever don a football helmet again.

Sinclair meets her on the field.

"You should have kicked the ball."

"I didn't want the kick to get blocked and the other team to run back for a touchdown."

"You could have had your pass picked off,"

She hadn't thought of that.

"You're right," she said.

"It was a hell of a pass!" He embraces his daughter, one of the few times he ever did, and whispers, "Never doubt yourself!"

She smiles and holds on tightly as tears stream down her face.

The following day, a video clip of the play was featured in the Sports Highlights of College Games. The announcer concludes by saying, "She should have just kicked the ball."

Enough already!

Chapter Five

IF YOU FOCUSED ON YOUR health as much as you did on one investment, you wouldn't be in this mess. You are putting a burden on Mom and the rest of us.

A nurse enters. "Hello, I am Nurse Amy. I will be taking care of your father."

Artemis meekly nods, "Thank you."

"He looks like he is having some discomfort, so I'm going to increase his morphine." After she administers the medication, she enters the information on the room computer. Artemis memorizes the keystrokes.

Two days later, Artemis receives a call from her mother.

"Your father is gone; they don't know what happened."

"It's OK, Mom. What's important is that we take care of you and move on as a family."

After she hangs up, she remembers her father's words, "Know when to cut them loose."

After the funeral, Delphi's Chief Operating Officer, John Stilwell, approaches Artemis.

"Your dad was a good man. We will get through this."

"Thanks, Uncle John." John Stilwell has worked with her father for many years. He knows the workings of the company better than her father did. Very methodical, more like obsessive-compulsive: "Everything has a place, even people." Artemis feels confident Stilwell will mentor her for the decisions she will soon have to make. Stilwell tells her that they will grow the company toward a bigger and better future.

The staff greets Artemis as she enters the Delphi Corporate Headquarters the following day. Many remember her as a child running down the halls and sitting at vacant cubicles drawing pictures with crayons. Now that her father has passed away, everyone seems eager to see the new direction the company will take. It does not take long before changes are made to the company with the acquisition of a humanoid-type robot manufacturing company, a small modular nuclear reactor company, and a cryogenic startup. Cost-cutting has become a daily routine, and notices are given to those in redundant positions. Some of the people had worked for the company for a long time. Business is business, Artemis declares, and a quick departure of employees is likely more beneficial for both the individuals and the company. She instructs supervisors to provide positive job reviews for departing employees. To further help them in their job search, she includes thirty days of job search assistance from an independent company.

Growth is taking place at a phenomenal pace, and Stilwell advises changing the corporate name from Delphi to Delphi Combined Industries to stand out as a major player. Further acquisitions in chip manufacture, quantum computing subsystems, and fusion energy systems propel DCI as one of the fastest-growing companies in the world.

Stilwell sits back in his office and marvels at the way he has been able to manipulate people and get what he wants. Like her father, Stilwell taps into Artemis' quest for power. When Sinclair originally started the business, Stilwell was there to provide compliments and confidence while at the same time sticking the knife in the boss's back.

He has been skimming funds from the company for years and has been making acquisitions of real estate under an assumed name. He has an accomplice in accounting who doctors the books. He has also hired people in the company to do work outside of their assigned duties under fictitious account numbers and funds his own secret research division, hiding it in plain sight. Like a chess master, Stilwell makes slow, deliberate moves. Things will happen when he wants them to. Artemis is but a pawn in his plan. She has the drive to make DCI the largest corporation in the world and will unknowingly fund Stilwell's personal ambitions.

Chapter Six

TONY WAKES UP IN A hospital bed; his head is pounding, his left hand is completely bandaged, and he sees his right leg has been amputated below the knee. He is groggy as hell and finds it difficult to concentrate.

"You're awake, good!" The doctor says to him, "You are at Ramstein Air Base, Germany; do you remember getting here?" He thinks back, "I remember the chopper."

"OK, that's good. You suffered some serious injuries, and we will do our best to get you back to health. Any questions?"

"Yeah, but I can't think of anything I want to know at this point."

"Nurse Jacobs will come in and take care of you."

Tony closes his eyes, trying to blink back the tears.

Hours later, a woman in a form-fitting business suit with high heels enters the hospital room. "Tony, Tony, thank God you're alive!"

"Hey, Kat. How did you get here?"

"I flew."

"Yeah, I know, but how did you get here so quickly? I know there has to be a lot of red tape."

"You do not want to know. Let's just say, I know people in high places."

"Yeah, I forgot you are the people person of the family," Tony remarks.

"Well, I have to do right by my little brother." Katherine Demarco-Martin was only three years older than Tony, but she was always protective of him. Like her mother, Kat is outgoing and strong-willed and looks like a replica of her Irish mother with her short brown hair and blue eyes.

"Are you in much pain?" she says.

"A little, they keep me doped up pretty good. I'm trying to get them to reduce the dose to at least just take the edge off."

"I was told you were the man of the hour."

"Not really; it was a team effort, and we were caught in a bad situation."

"You saved a little girl who is at the Children's Hospital."

"Yeah, about that; hey, Kat, sit down. Let's talk."

Tony briefly goes over what he was doing in the past twelve months and the interactions he has had with Hassan and his family, leaving out parts his sister probably wouldn't want to hear.

"Mina has been through enough; she doesn't deserve this. She has lost too much. She's lost her parents and brother. And now she endures pain from losing her leg. Kat, we have to help her."

Overcome with emotion, he cries as his sister holds him tight just like when they were kids. Kat was always the fixer in the family. Unlike people who would utter trite expressions at business meetings like, "Let's find a pathway to yes," Kat would get things done no matter what the obstacle. Keeping her brother safe and happy is now at the top of her list. "Just let it out," Kat says. "We will see what we can do."

Katherine DeMarco was the glue that held the family together. Her father lingered with lung cancer for six months. She would take him to chemo treatment when Mom had to work. Kat had good grades but had to curtail activities after school to help Mom. Kat was aware of the family's plan to relocate to Virginia after her father's death, and while it was not unexpected, it was nonetheless devastating. She felt guilty. Kat was sad that her father died but relieved now that they could start a new life in a new state. She liked living in Hope Mills, a few miles from Fort Bragg, but it was time to move on. She convinced Tony that the change of surroundings would be good. She was finishing her senior year, and the family moved to Virginia right after she graduated from high school. She was accepted into a Northern Virginia college and excelled in all her classes. She joined the women's lacrosse team, where she received a few bruises but handed them out as well. She was passionate at times, and the gloves came off when she got into it with players from other teams. But after the game, she abandoned all aggression and left it on the field. She was well liked by her teammates. She graduated with a business degree, then pursued an MBA, and eventually earned a degree in corporate law. Kat was in high demand and worked as an intern on Capitol Hill for several agencies before turning to the private sector, where she made real money. She would handle problems when members of Congress or senators over-promised their constituents or approved contracts where there was a perceived or actual organizational conflict of interest. Kat was a fixer. She was a straight shooter and didn't break any laws but occasionally would bend them. Unlike her mother, who wore her emotions on her sleeve, Kat would keep them in check and would release them when the occasion arrived.

Kat visits Tony once more. True to her word, she calls in every favor from the Department of State, Congress, and the Consulate. Mina is a refugee, and she is awarded special consideration. Kat manages to pull strings that will allow Mina to transfer to the Washington, DC, Children's Hospital. Tony will not be far away since he will be flown to Andrews Air Force Base and will be moved to Walter Reed in Maryland.

"I'm leaving, but I will visit you once you get settled in at Walter Reed."

"How is Mom taking it?"

"You know, Mom, she doesn't want anything to happen to her favorite child." They both laugh; it has always been an ongoing joke who was the *favorite* child. "Anyway, I will be bringing Mom. I will tell her to behave herself and not to get overly emotional, but we are talking about Mom, and you know how that goes."

A day later, they take Tony to the airfield and load him onto a military aircraft bound for Andrews Air Force Base. Upon his arrival, an ambulance transports him to Walter Reed Hospital, where a crowd of well-wishers eagerly awaits his recovery. He settles into a room, feeling relieved to be back in the US. He turns on the TV. He is amazed major news reports are more concerned with the lives of celebrities and professional athletes and feel-good stories than with what is going on in the rest of the world. The events that occurred in Afghanistan receive only about thirty seconds of coverage.

So much for news. He turns off the TV.

Soon Kat comes in with Mom.

"What have they done to my son!" She bursts into tears.

"It's OK, Mom, I'm alright."

"You don't look alright; are you in pain?"

"Only when I laugh," and then Tony laughs. Mom lightly hits him on the shoulder.

"You are always joking; you never take anything seriously. His mom knows him well; he is able to cope with the worst of times by using humor.

"I'm sorry, Anthony, I didn't mean it."

"It's OK, Mom." She hugs and kisses her son.

Mom sits down and gets Tony up to date on the family. Uncle Bill has been storing Tony's motorcycle in the garage and has been keeping the battery charged. He has even ridden it around, much to the dismay of Aunt Mary. Then she discusses the cousins, which ones are getting married, and who is having a baby.

"Kat, did you tell Mom about—?" Kat stops him mid-sentence.

"About what?" His mother says.

"Mom, Tony needs to get some rest. Let's go grab a coffee downstairs in the cafeteria."

"What is so secret that you had to drag me down here?" Mom asks.

Kat says, "OK, how do I say it? Mom, you are going to be a grandmother."

"Oh, Katherine, you're pregnant!"

"No, I'm not pregnant; this is going to be a long story." Kat tells Mom about Mina and how Tony saved the little girl's life and the promise that he made to her father.

"No, he has done too much already; no one expects him to raise a daughter in his condition." Kat waits and lets her mother vent. Mom and Kat go back upstairs and talk a little more to Tony, who is nodding off at this point, and they avoid the subject of raising Mina.

Kat finally says, "This is important to Tony; we can make it work." Kat convinces her mother to go to the Children's Hospital with her.

Upon their arrival, the nurses take them to the room. "She looks so helpless," Mom says and places her hand close to the little girl. Mina, who has been drifting in and out of consciousness due to the drugs, opens her eyes and grabs Mom's hand. Overcome with emotion, she looks up. "I have a granddaughter," and she smiles.

Chapter Seven

"YOU OK?" THE MALE NURSE says. "Breakfast will come in a few minutes; you have physical therapy in an hour." Tony looks at the bleak day outside in Bethesda, Maryland.

A knock at the door "Hey, are you up for a guest?"

"You aren't a guest; you're just another inmate just like me," Tony says.

"Not anymore." Major Michael Albert Collins, also known as Mac, replies.

"And what did you do to get a reprieve? Wait, never mind, I don't want to know."

They both laugh. Mac says,

"My TBI (traumatic brain injury) has gotten better, my memory is intact, and my balance has improved quite a bit. I can lose the cane in a couple of months." Tony smiles.

"That's great. I'm glad you are recovering nicely."

"Well, you seem to be getting better as well."

"Not as quickly as you, but I'm not complaining."

Mac hands him a package.

"Well, I got something here for you; it's from the team and me."

"Please tell me it's not another puzzle."

"Yeah, we thought about it," Mac laughs.

Tony opens up a new tablet computer.

"Hey, thanks; this is great. Tell the guys thanks as well."

"Tony, I figured you could read a little better without having to turn pages, and you can surf the internet. Sure beats using your cell phone."

Mac gives Tony an update on everything that is going on in the unit and in their world. He tells Tony who is leaving, who is switching teams, and who are retiring out. They speak for a few minutes about family and friends and upcoming medical procedures.

"Well, brother, time for me to pop smoke; looks like they're bringing you your breakfast." Mac leaves, giving a firm handshake and a slap on the shoulder.

"See you, Tony."

"Take care, Mac. See you back at Bragg."

Mac was team leader on Tony's (Special Forces Operational Detachment "A"), or 'A team,' when he was the detachment senior engineer sergeant. Mac did his best to avoid getting picked up for a staff job and managed to stay on the team for three years. He liked life on an A-Team, and even when he became company commander, he was never far from the team room. He liked action. While growing up in Oklahoma, he worked on a ranch and enjoyed the rewards of hard work. He went to college and attained a degree in aeronautical engineering with the hopes of being a pilot for the Air Force, the Navy, or the Marines, but uncorrected vision dashed those hopes. He joined the Army with the intent of joining Special Forces, succeeded in achieving that goal, and also obtained his private pilot license.

Seeing his friend and his company commander leave, Tony is more determined to get well. He goes to physical therapy, but even the simplest task takes more effort than he realizes. He obsesses over his recovery and recalls a commonly used saying. "Pain is just weakness leaving the body." He tries to convince himself of that, but he soon realizes pain just 'sucks.' He guts through the exercises. By the end of the session, he is sweating profusely and is clearly agitated.

"Let's run through this again; I can do better," Tony says.

"Sorry, Sergeant DeMarco, get some rest, and we will schedule another appointment for you tomorrow."

Tony slides onto the wheelchair and is taken back to his room. Frustrated, he closes his eyes and remembers a time when he had a nagging injury to his back.

His wife, Gina, who was watching a yoga video, says,

"Why don't you give it a try? You may feel better." Reluctant at first, he says,

"What the hell, I'll give it a try."

After 10 minutes he feels better than he had in months and would practice the same routine from time to time, even during deployments. He had a good thing with Gina. They were a great couple, both in love. But back-to-back deployments that start in months and turn to years make it hard on a marriage. Special Forces is a cruel mistress, but the marriage ends on amicable terms.

Tony goes online searching for yoga videos. He enters a search, 'Doing Yoga in a Hospital Bed,' and to his surprise, he finds dozens of videos. He finds a quote: "If you can breathe, you can do yoga." He starts a video, and in ten minutes he is in a restful sleep. He needs it.

Over the next several weeks he quickly improves following each physical therapy session with a few minutes of yoga.

Kat picks up Greg at Reagan Airport, and they stop and have lunch. She knows Greg is Tony's best friend, and he is definitely a little awkward, but she could see he is a true friend to her brother. Greg had been a star quarterback in high school and a straight 'A' student. He had aspirations of getting into Louisiana State University and being an LSU Tiger until he blew out his knee in November of his senior year. With a scholarship off the table, his parents still wanted him to go to college and suggested going to a Historically Black College, but he declined. He was into electronics and computers and opted to go to a two-year college, getting an associate degree in electrical engineering, and he was eventually drawn to the military. Greg and Tony had been through a lot together and always had each other's back.

Greg and Kat enter the hospital room. "What's up, Brother? Greg says.

"Kat, what did I tell you about this guy? He's a phenom."

"So, Tony tells me you have a photographic memory."

"I don't know about that. Oh, wait a second, what's today's date? Oh yeah, the twenty-first. OK, last year we were in Brussels. Tony, you had the quiche Lorraine, and I had the soufflé."

Tony laughs, "No, I had the soufflé."

Kat says, "Really?"

"No. Never been to Brussels, we're just pulling your leg."

Kat rolls her eyes and shakes her head. Greg says, "I just have good short-term memory, and I can remember three sets of phone numbers at one time and random objects in a photo in a few seconds of seeing it. The kids at grade school hated me for finding the differences in two pictures; I always finished first. Well, so much about me. Hey, Tony, we're breaking you out of this place!" Kat glares at Greg and clarifies,

"Not exactly; we are temporarily taking you out to see Mina at the Children's Hospital for compassionate reasons."

"How did you manage that?"

"It's a long story, but don't be surprised if you see the press there."

"You leveraged the press?"

"Well, yes, and possibly some members of Congress."

Greg asks, "Hey, if I ever get in trouble, will you be my attorney?"

"Sorry. I'm a contract attorney. Trial law is not in my wheelhouse."

After a short drive, they arrive at the hospital; Tony is on crutches. As he breathes outside air again, *it feels good to be wearing jeans.*

They walk up to the nurses station, and the nurse introduces herself. "We are concerned; Mina cries often and refuses to eat or speak to anyone."

They step inside the room, and the little girl averts her eyes. "Mina, we brought someone here that you know. As soon as she looks up, she yells, "Mister Tony, Mister Tony!" She opens her arms for a hug. Tony holds her tight. She cries tears of joy, and at last she feels safe. Greg and Aunt Kat hug her as well. Tony sees her uneaten lunch and says, "Let's eat, princess," pointing toward the tray.

"What is a princess?" Tony opens a picture book that they brought. He picks it up and points to the princess in the story. He then says, "You are the princess, Princess Mina."

"Princess Mina!" She says and smiles.

"You are a princess," Kat replies as she wipes the tears from her eyes.

As they visit with Mina, photographers come into the room and take quick pictures of Tony and Mina. The nurse pushes the photographers out the door and closes it.

"Sorry, we are not used to having celebrities here."

"We're not celebrities."

"You are today!"

They say goodbye to Mina and walk through the gauntlet of photographers. When they return Tony to his room, the TV is on. They're all over the local DC news.

Chapter Eight

AS HE CHECKS IN FOR his flight to Reagan, the TSA agent hands him back his ID and says, "Have a good flight, Mr. Siegel." Nick Siegel is tall and thin; his black hair is thinning, and he wears black-rimmed glasses like he has most of his life, what his friends refer to as anti-rape glasses. He boards the flight and eases into his seat, looking forward to seeing his best friend, Tony. He calls Kat to say he will be there in about four hours and asks about Tony. He thinks about how he first met Tony in sophomore year at high school. A group of jocks bullies Nick while he's carrying his lunch tray. They start pulling things off his tray and then trip him. Nick falls flat. The jocks start kicking him. Then they hear a voice.

"Let him alone." It is Tony Demarco, all of one hundred and twenty-five pounds and just over five feet tall.

"What are you going to do?"

Tony doesn't respond but helps Nick get up. The biggest kid gets in front of Tony and says,

"How about I kick your ass? Tony looks him straight in the eye and says,

"Yeah, why don't you start practicing falling down first?"

This causes a collective response, 'Oo-Oo-Oo,' and then the crowd starts laughing. The kid pushes Tony, and the two other jocks start pushing him from the sides. Tony doesn't fall for it and focuses on the leader. Tony charges forward, grabs the kid by the collar, and delivers six brutal punches to the leader's face, drawing blood from the kid's mouth. The crowd is silent. The gym teacher grabs the beaten kid and Tony and marches them to the principal's office. Nick remembers that day like it was yesterday.

After Tony's suspension, no one messed with him or any of his friends.

"Why do you always have to be the hero?" his mom says.

"Was it a smaller kid they were picking on?"

"No, but there were three of them."

"So you decided to fight all three at the same time."

"I only had to hit the first one, and the other two backed off."

"Tony, Please try and not get into any more fights. I cannot afford to take any more time
off from work."

"OK, Mom." She knows that Tony will help anyone without hesitation. Tony and Nick soon became fast friends and would remain close ever since. Nick would see Tony run track, and Tony would watch Nick compete in robot competitions.

As Nick enters the hospital room, he sees Tony is resting.

"Hey, stranger, how's it going?"

"Nick, what are you doing here? Last I heard, you were moving to Arizona."

"I did. I started working for DCI, or I should say Delphi Combined Industries."

"You flew out all that way to see me."

"Well, for you and the job. I have to go to corporate and meet with the rest of the people assigned to Space Systems."

"Space Systems? Are you flying rockets to the moon?" Tony says jokingly.

"Not yet, just designing them."

"Wow, that's great."

"It's OK. It puts food on the table." Nick says with a smile. Nick has always been humble, and he is likable.

"How about you?" he tells Tony.

"I saw you on the news with that little girl. It said the hero saved a little girl in Afghanistan. It's all over the news!"

"Yeah, well, you can't believe everything you see on the news," they both laugh.

"How is Julie?"

"She's doing well. Julie is five months pregnant! She told me, I better see the best man from the wedding, or don't bother coming home!" They both laugh and talk about the good time they had at Nick's wedding. They reminisce about trips they took together; and other fun times they had. Tony tells Nick about Mina and what had occurred in Afghanistan. They talk for several hours.

"Well, I have to go to a meeting. Duty calls."

"Take care, thanks for coming."

"You take care! Love you, Brother." Nick gives him a fist bump as he leaves

Later, the nurse comes in the room saying,

"How is our star patient? It is all over the news how a soldier saved an Afghani child."

"I did not expect this much attention."

"You deserve it; enjoy the moment."

The next two days, lines of people come to see him. He receives gratitude from legislators, military personnel, and entertainers for his heroism and service. He prides himself on being a 'quiet professional.' A motto attributed to Special Forces. He really doesn't want the added attention. "Just doing my job," he says. After the people leave, Tony asks,

"Can I get out of here for the weekend or at least one day?"

"I'll check with the doctor," the nurse responds.

The doctor enters the room.

"You have surgery next Thursday. I'll tell you what, you can go Saturday morning at eight am, but you need to get back by four pm on Sunday." He pauses.

"That's the best I can do. I have to follow orders just like you."

"OK, thanks, I'll make it work," Tony says with a wry smile.

He has Kat bring him some clothes. She brings a herringbone overcoat from her ex and buys Tony a set of black sneakers.

"This is all I could get on short notice," Kat says.

"This will work." Tony wants to dress incognito, no military garb.

"Are you sure you would rather not stay with me or Mom?"

"No, I just need to get out and walk around, hit the museums, go to a comedy club, and maybe get a drink."

"I'll drop you off; you call me when you want to get picked up, OK? You're not going with any friends?"

"No, I just want to take a day away from the Army. I just don't want to talk about work or deployments."

"I can appreciate it; everyone needs to get away from work for a while." Tony puts on the coat, which is way too big. Kat's husband was over six feet two and much heavier. Tony is five feet seven with a trim build.

I must look ridiculous with this coat and watch cap.

"Does this make me look distinguished?" Kat laughs.

"Sure, let's go with that." It doesn't matter; he is glad to get out. He stopped using the crutches a couple of days ago, and he is able to walk better now that he has places to go. He goes to the Air and Space Museum and the Museum of Natural History, checks out the Art Museum, and eats a late lunch in the cafeteria. It is good getting out, and he enjoys just sitting down and eating at a table even though the food isn't the best. He grabs a cab and checks in at the hotel. He lies down for a few hours watching a car auction show. He later goes to a comedy club and stops for a drink at a club just off of Pennsylvania Avenue. A young woman starts talking to him and asks him where he works. Using a cover story, he says, "I work for the government as an analyst." She is talkative, and he likes just hearing carefree chatter. He goes to the bar to get two drinks. When he returns with the drinks, she notices his limp and gloved hand, which clearly dampens the mood of the conversation. They finish their drinks, and he says, "It was great talking with you," and leaves with a simple handshake. Feeling hungry, he checks his phone for nearby restaurants and discovers a sports bar. It's not very crowded, and he gets a hamburger since he doesn't want to try cutting a steak with his injured hand. He decides to walk off the big meal and walks up 10th Street. He sees three guys up to no good, so he crosses to the other side. "Hey, where are you going?" They step in front of him.

Oh, shit! I don't need this.

"Where are you going?" the 'leader' says.

"Just going home," Tony says.

"You don't want to talk to us." They all had their hands in their pockets; he knew they had guns. They see he had a bulge in the pocket of his overcoat.

"What's that?"

"Just a can of nuts," Tony says. He always carries snacks.

"Let's see it." He pulls it out to show them. One of the other guys starts laughing. "Look at that, he has his nuts in a can." Tony laughs as well, trying to diffuse the situation. "Shut up!" The leader pulls out a Glock-style ghost gun, holding the barrel sideways like thugs in the movies, aiming at Tony's head.

"How about I put a cap in your ass?"

Tony stands there and closes his eyes. *I guess the fun time is over.*

"Hey, you hear me!" he hits Tony on top of the head with the barrel

"Look, I don't have anything." He flips the cap off the can. "But Nuts!"

He throws the contents up in the air, and as they look up, he goes into a crouch and takes out the knee of the leader, then comes up from behind him and slams his foot down, forcing the thug's bent knee down with force. He doesn't try to take the gun; instead, he grabs the bottom of the gun with his right hand and twists the thug's hand 180 degrees.

"Let go, you're breaking my wrist." The two other guys take out their ghost guns, and Tony glares at them and says, "Don't." As they raise their barrels, Tony uses the palm of his left hand to push down the trigger finger of the leader, who is unable to release his grip. He lets off two shots, not hitting the other two thugs even though he could have done so easily. They take off running blindly, firing high behind them.

He pulls the gun away from the leader.

"Don't kill me," he pleads.

"Not today, you piece of shit!"

Tony hits him with the gun on the side of the face, and the thug lies in pain in a fetal position. Tony has seen enough death; he doesn't need to add to the numbers.

Tony is pumped. He runs and skips, covering a couple of blocks in no time, and as soon as he sees no one is behind him, he checks the gun and marvels at how well it is made and the detail of the 3D-printed parts. He finds a fast food bag, puts the gun in it, and drops it in one of the last drop boxes for the post office in the District of Columbia. *The police can lift fingerprints and handle it as they see fit.* He walks to Freedom Plaza and looks back at the brightly lit Capitol building in the distance. Enjoying the crisp air, he walks back to the hotel and gets a good night's rest.

Chapter Nine

THE NEXT DAY, KAT PICKS him up at the hotel.

"Did you have a good time? Did you stay out of trouble?"

"Always," he says. She knows better; *trouble always has a way of finding him.* "Take care. Do you meet with the surgeon tomorrow?"

"Yes, they are going to explain the procedure."

As he gets out of the car, he says,

"Thanks, Kat, I owe you."

"Yep, I'll add it to your tab." Tony goes up to the room and settles in for the night. It has been a busy two days. He hasn't done this much moving around in a while. He is worn out but relaxed. The doctor meets him in his room the following morning.

"Did you have a good day out?"

"It was great, very therapeutic."

"Good, I hope you didn't overdo it."

"No, I took it slow," Tony says.

"Yeah, I kind of doubt that, but I'm glad you had a good time." The doctor says.

"We are going to operate on your hand on Thursday. I know you have some medical training, so here is the X-ray." The doctor shows him the X-ray on a tablet.

"We are going to repair the two metacarpals on your left hand using titanium plates called t-minis to reinforce the bones. The procedure will promote healing and will give you full use of your palm."

"How about two new fingers while you're at it?" Tony jokes.

"I'm glad you haven't lost your sense of humor. But the remaining parts of the two fingers will give you some function and will help with the grip strength."

"By the way, when can I be released?" Tony asks.

"In about 10 days, depending on the surgery, and then we can start seeing you as an outpatient."

"Great, I can't wait." He calls Kat and tells her the news.

"Tony, I'm so happy for you. Someone else will be happy. It looks like Mina can leave the hospital sometime next month."

"Kat, I know this is a lot to dump on you."

"Yeah, I know; you will be staying with me for a while."

"You were always a mind reader," Tony says.

"Don't worry, big sister has your back." Things are looking up.

He undergoes the surgery, and the doctor comes in while he is in recovery.

"The operation went exceptionally well." We were able to reinforce the damaged area, and you should get quite a bit of function back. We reduced the previous scarring, so you will get movement back in about ten days. You still have a lot of healing to do, but keep the positive attitude."

Tony thinks back to the ghost gun and starts reading everything he can find on the Internet about 3D printing. He is amazed at how well 3D printers work and how simple it is to get started. He finds thousands of designs on the websites. Many people design their own prints for everything from gadgets for the home, superhero costumes and accessories, and precision-engineered parts and assemblies. Other people design toys, various storage solutions, or general life hacks. He wants to make things that are functional, and he finds a free computer-aided drafting program that allows you to design objects using preloaded shapes. Tony is amazed at how intricately he could design something on his tablet. He starts taking free courses on material science and engineering, quickly advancing his skill set.

Tony begins physical therapy. A week later his hand is healing well, and a smaller dressing is applied. The doctor assesses Tony's range of motion and expresses satisfaction with the results, leading to his release from the hospital a few days later. Kat picks him up.

"How did it go?"

"It went really well. I have good range of motion and will get back most of my hand strength."

"Great, I am glad things are going well. I will put you in the spare bedroom."

"Thanks, Kat, you're the best."

Several days later, he asks Kat if he can use her other car. Kat has a hatchback that she drives in tight areas where she doesn't want to take the SUV.

"How are you going to drive with your right foot?"

"I figured it out. I can drive with my left foot; I just need to adjust the seat."

"Please be careful."

"Don't worry, I'm just going to see Mom and Uncle Bill."

Tony enjoys getting on the road, not having to be chauffeured everywhere he has to go. He finds the forty-five-minute drive relaxing; he misses driving. Still, he has to keep the visit short; he isn't ready to drive during the rush hour. Fortunately, the car has active cruise control, so it is easier to drive than expected.

"Hi, Mom," he says as he walks through the door.

"Your sister told me you were coming," Mom says.

"You shouldn't be driving."

"It's fine, no problem. Just trying to get a sense of normalcy."

He sits down for a long time with Mom and discusses the future. How are they going to integrate Mina into the family?

"Mom, when Mina gets released from the hospital, we will move in with you for a short time. I still don't know what my status is until I get back to Fort Bragg."

"Don't worry, Anthony, we will work it out." They discuss tentative plans, but the likelihood is that the plans will change considerably. They walk down the street and visit with Uncle Bill and Aunt Mary. They have always been supportive of Tony and wrote to him during long deployments. Like his father, Uncle Bill was in the military. He served in the Air Force and traveled extensively. He left after six years; the private sector paid very well with fewer hours. Now retired, he enjoys his life and still works out and stays active.

"Hey, Uncle Bill, let's go in the garage." Tony wants to talk to someone who could appreciate what he is going through and not overwhelm him with sympathy. Uncle Bill could talk straight to him.

"Tony, you have been an action guy for a long time. At some point that is going to end."

"I realize that. If I can manage for a couple more years, I can do my twenty years."

"You know, if you get medically discharged, they will pay you your full retirement benefits."

"I get it, but I want to leave on a high note." Uncle Bill smiles.

"We all want to leave on a high note. Just don't anticipate what might happen; keep a positive attitude. There are plenty of contracting jobs available; you might find them rewarding." They discuss various options. Tony appreciates the insights from his uncle.

Tony says, "Let's look at the bike." Uncle Bill has been storing the motorcycle for two years and has taken meticulous care of it, leaving it on a battery tender and running it every so often. He takes care of it much better than Tony. After he straddles the bike, he realizes he can't quite grasp the clutch. "Let's adjust that." Uncle Bill gets some tools. It feels good just to sit on the bike. It will be a little time before he can ride again, if ever. "The foot brake will be a problem."

"Don't worry, give it time. You will get back on the bike again." Uncle Bill has ridden bikes for a long time and understands Tony's passion for riding.

They spend the rest of the time swapping stories.

"You can't make this stuff up," Uncle Bill says, and they laugh at some of the experiences they both had in the military. They go back into the house, and Tony spends time with Aunt Mary and Mom before he leaves.

When he gets back, Kat says,

"You have a package. Did you order something?"

"Yes, a new hobby," he says with a wry smile.

"I will be working tonight, so there is food in the refrigerator if you're hungry."

When Kat leaves, he opens the package and starts working. He has his tablet open to a CAD program and is taking measurements with a digital caliper. He is still at it when Kat comes back later in the evening.

"What are you making? Is that a gun?"

"Yeah, it's a Glock knockoff; I'm redesigning it."

"To shoot." Kat asks.

"Eventually, the intent is to get well versed in 3D printing. I have been taking a couple of engineering courses online. I'm starting with this so I can design a grip to shoot with either hand, and I'm making a swing-away trigger guard."

"Boys with their toys, don't let Mom see you with that."

Chapter Ten

A MONTH LATER, KAT, Mom, and Tony are walking through the doors of Children's Hospital. Mom says,

"I still don't understand how you did it, but Mina is coming with us."

"Yes, we are working through the red tape to get approval for adoption." Mina is a refugee, and that counts for a lot of assistance. Since this is a unique circumstance and there has been so much media coverage, it was easier to push through. A little help from members of Congress did not hurt either," Kat says.

They stop by the nurses' station and head up to Mina's room. She is excited to see Kat and Tony. Kat says,

"You're coming home with us today."

"Yes," Mina squeals with delight.

"Here is something for you, princess." Tony gives her a shiny tiara with a green plastic gem. The nurse comes in and says, "Wow, what a beautiful tiara."

"I'm a princess," Mina says in delight.

The nurse plays along.

"Well, princess, you are getting released today, and the doctor is coming in to check on you so you can go home.

"Home?" Mina says. Mom says,

"Yes, Mina, you are going to live with us." Kat drives through the city, and Mina is fascinated by the monuments and buildings. As they cross the 14th Street bridge, Mina points and says, "Ocean?"

Tony smiles. "Not an ocean but a river." Mina is amazed; being in a landlocked country, she had never seen a large body of water. "Some day soon we will go to the ocean."

When they get to the house, Mina is not accustomed to these living standards. Though she likes 'her room,' she is not used to living in comfort and is unsure how to play with the toys she is given. Mina is not familiar with toys that use batteries, but she settles on holding the baby doll that the nurses gave her at the hospital. She is slowly getting acquainted with American life, but the popular cartoons are too frenetic. So Mom puts Mina on her lap and reads from a picture book. She is able to pick up words rapidly, and she is having fun learning new things. Mom keeps a supply of crafts Mina can work on. Eventually, Mom finds some calmer programming, and Mina enjoys watching a British cartoon, and she starts to develop a British accent when imitating the words she hears on the show. Aunt Kat thinks it is hilarious when Mina asks,

"Can we go on holiday?" Kat answers,

"Of course we can. Mina, you're a quick learner!"

Two weeks later they plan a trip to Virginia Beach. Kat wasn't going to go at first, but she anticipates an outcome that Tony does not consider. As they travel by car, Mina is nervous about how fast cars and trucks travel on the expressway. She is frightened by the large expanse of water while traveling over the bridge. Mina starts crying, holding tight to Mom, who tries to comfort her. They had booked a suite at a high-rise hotel with an ocean view. They enter the room, and Tony leads Mina to the balcony. Mina lets out a heart-stopping scream. Kat picks her up and brings her back to the room. Tony asks,

"What's wrong?"

"What's wrong?!" Kat says with an edge. "How many fifteen-story buildings are in Afghanistan? And for that matter, what ocean is in Afghanistan? Tony, she is a little girl who is in culture shock and only understands less than a quarter of what we say."

"I'm sorry, I guess I am showing her too much too fast." Both Mom and Kat look at Tony and nod. They let Mina take a nap. When she wakes up, they keep things simple and introduce Mina to fast food, getting her a kids' meal from a burger chain. After a day filled with excitement, they sit by the pool to allow Mina to watch the kids splashing and playing in the water.

The next day Kat dresses Mina in a bathing suit, and they walk to the beach. Mina is not afraid at first, but as she gets closer and sees the waves crashing, she becomes scared and squeezes Tony's neck so tightly that she chokes him.

"Mina, not so tight; I won't let you go," Tony says. As soon as he walks in two feet of water again, she squeezes his neck, yelling, "No, no, no." Tony walks with Mina back on the beach. Auntie Kat takes over walking on the beach with Mina and walking towards the water when the waves pull back. After a time, Mina would hold Tony's hand with one hand, and Kat would hold Mina's other hand. They would lift Mina up when a wave came in, allowing her to feel the rush of the water, which made her laugh. Kat says,

"It's all about trust; she will get used to it." They take her by the pool without her prosthetic, and she is able to move pretty well, holding on to the side of the pool. She meets other children who accept her like any other kid.

In the following weeks, the bond grows stronger between Tony and Mina. She enjoys learning new things, and Tony does as well, buying a 3D printer and designing different things, mostly related to prosthetics and performance-enhancing designs. Tony is improving each day and enjoys the time off spent with Mom and Mina. Then reality sets in.

What am I going to do? Do I have to take a medical retirement? Do I have to be on permanent disability and work staff jobs for the next three years? He does not want to be a REMF (rear echelon MF'er). Maybe he could get an exception to policy and be deployable, but it is a long shot. He is getting depressed. The worst thing that comes to mind is being non-deployable. Like most of the team guys, it is a love-hate relationship. You hate the long days, the austere conditions, being away from your family, and giving up your freedom to do anything but mission stuff when deployed. But he loves the challenges of doing things you could never do anywhere else, going to places you'd never go outside of the military, and being part of something bigger than yourself.

He looks at his phone for hours and finally decides to call his friends.

"Hey Greg, how is it going?"

"OK, not too much going on, except inventories, briefings, and ceremonies."

"So I'm not missing anything." Tony says.

"Not too much until next month... How's it going with you?"

Greg listens as Tony describes the fight, the ghost gun, and the quality of its construction. Tony talks to him for a long time about physical therapy, taking college courses, and getting into 3D printing. He talks about Mina and how well she is doing, aside from the cultural shock of living in America.

"Man, that's great! I'm glad you're not sitting around and getting drunk. If you need anything, I'm here for you. Call up Mac on his cell; he is transitioning out of the company, but he wants to talk to you."

A couple of hours later, he calls Mac.

"I've been waiting for you to call." Mac says,

"Greg told me you were moving out of the company," Tony replies.

"I'm getting promoted."

"Congratulations." They discuss at length how he is doing and how Mina is adjusting. Finally, Tony comes to the end of the chase.

"Am I getting a medical discharge?"

"Only. If you want one."

"Not me, I want to stay in," Tony says.

"Great!" Look, can you be back in four weeks? I'm putting a team together."

"What kind of team?"

"Something brand new, a good opportunity. I can't go into it right now; I'm still working on the details. I will email you what I can; it may be a reassignment. Don't worry, it will be Special Ops."

Tony says, "OK, thanks."

"You take care; I owe you."

Tony is intrigued and later receives an email from Mac with links to Space Force and the Special Operations Liaison Element to USSPACECOM. As promised, Tony returns to Fort Bragg and catches up with friends. He stops by the team room.

"Look who the cat dragged in," Tommy Thompson says.

"Hey, Brother, good to see you too. That was some shooting, at least that's what I was told; I couldn't see much from my vantage point."

"Understandable, glad to see you in the vertical." Tony laughs at that one. Tommy is always good for comic relief, no matter the circumstances. Tony meets Gabriel (Gabe) Suarez, the medic that worked on him. They talk for a while. Gabe says,

"How is the little girl, Mina?"

"She is getting better every day; you know I adopted her."

"Man, that's great. There was something on the news about you visiting her. Great to see you again."

Tony goes to Lieutenant Colonel Collins' office.

"Morning, Colonel."

"Thanks, I'm still trying to get used to that title. Yes, I need to maintain military courtesy now that we are back in garrison; I hope this doesn't last long. When was your last flight physical?"

"About a year and a half ago, why?"

"You saw the stuff I sent you?"

"I did, but I'm still puzzled."

"Good, so am I. We are setting up a Special Forces Mobile Training Team to integrate with elements of the Space Force."

"Aren't they out in Colorado?"

"They are, but we are going to operate out of Hurlburt Field."

"So what's the flight physical for? Am I going to the moon?" Mac laughs.

"No, but how would you like to go back to jump status?"

"Not if it's a static line."

"No, you will be back on HALO (High Altitude Low Opening). I signed you up for the Wind Tunnel. You'll be going there for the next three days. The instructors are going to run you through the paces like you never did this before since your injuries have probably affected your flight dynamics."

"Great, I have to start somewhere." He understands that he needs to reacquaint himself with the wind tunnel.

"This will not be a temporary duty assignment; it will be a permanent change of station. In the meantime, you have to do some of those admin things. Check in with Battalion Supply; you have some things to pick up. Also, touch base with the Battalion Ops. Before you do anything else, you need to see the command sergeant major and the battalion commander, group commander, and whoever else they want you to meet. You are a popular person around here."

When Tony returns, he attends an award ceremony. He attends an award ceremony. He receives a Silver Star and a Purple Heart for actions taken during that fateful day in Afghanistan and receives huge applause. He again meets with Chief Mike Wilcox, who is walking with assistance. This will be Mike's last day in the Army; he is getting medically retired.

"Tony, you saved Mac and me that day. I appreciate what you did. Without that warning, we wouldn't have been able to get down on the ground before the explosion."

"I appreciate what you did, Chief. We are a team." Tony gives him a salute, and Chief smiles and salutes back. Tony shakes hands with him and all the others and goes in for refreshments and snacks. Greg, Gabe, and Tommy receive Bronze Stars as well. The festivities end, and then it's back to the normal busywork, all part of being a soldier.

Death by paperwork.

He has to go to legal, then back to Admin to get Mina put on as a dependent, but she doesn't have a birth certificate. Finally, over two days, he gets everything worked out.

Tony shows up to the wind tunnel for training. He has done this before, but his body geometry has changed, and he has to relearn this skill. Changes to his hand and leg make it difficult. Although frustrated, by the third day he feels confident in his skills. He can fly flat, dumb, and happy; flips are definitely out right now. He is able to get in three jumps and is confident in his abilities. He reports back to Mac and lets him know he is back up to speed. "See you down in Florida."

When he gets back to Virginia, he tells Mom of the plan. They will be moving to Florida. Tony finds a suitable house close to the base for rent on the Internet. Kat arranges the move-in and turns on the utilities. There is a long list of things he has to do, and Uncle Bill helps him to get Mom's house ready as a rental property.

Chapter Eleven

IN FLORIDA, MOM, MINA, and Tony move into a rental house, and they are finally able to get on a routine. Mina finds a girl about her age living next door. Mina and the girl, Molly, become close friends, and they play well together. Life is good.

The assignment is better than expected, and Tony looks forward to new challenges. He is set up in a team room at Hurlburt Field and starts attending with the Space Force personnel, who are called 'Guardians.' It is different, low-key. He doesn't mind it, and he gets off at a reasonable time. Tony arrives home,

"Hi, Mom. Where's Mina? She's in her room crying."

He walks in, "Come on, princess, what's wrong? You can tell me."

"A boy called me Cyborg. He says your daddy is Cyborg too."

Mom has tears in her eyes. This really makes Tony think he has been going too fast. He wasn't so bent out of shape that a kid called her names but never took the time to explain the relationship; he is still Mr. Tony or Tony. He looks to Mom. "I can use your help." Mom agrees.

"I have an idea; let's go for ice cream," Tony says.

"Anthony Robert!" His mother says. "We will be right back, Mina,"

"Tony, you can't do that; you have to solve the problem, not gloss over it. Ice cream doesn't solve everything. She doesn't understand the relationship; she thinks you are just a friend to her father."

"You are right, Mom. I'm no good with this stuff."

"You just need to relax; you can't power through every problem. You have to take things as they come. Mina is a little girl; you have to give her time to adjust."

"Yes, Mom." Tony goes back to the bedroom and sits on the bed. Mom watches from the doorway.

Mina dries her eyes and rubs her nose.

"Your papa, Hasan, was like a brother to me. I promised him I would take care of you. So you are like a 'lour' or daughter to me."

Tony points to himself and then points to Mina; she nods yes. Tony touches Mom's hand; Mina has been calling her Mom as well.

"You can call her Bibi." Mom nods.

"You can call me Daddy, or Dad, or Tony if you want."

"OK, Daddy or Dad." Mom and Tony both laugh.

They finally agree on the title of 'Daddy.' He asks Mom,

"Are you up for shopping?" She knows where this conversation is going and says yes. Tony realizes he can't shield his daughter forever and doesn't want her to be a victim or even think she is. Tony takes them to the mall, and they get some ice cream, and then he lets Mom and Mina get some alone time. Mina has been wearing long pants that cover her prosthetic leg. Now she doesn't have to hide it; she has potential. After they go clothes shopping, they go to the toy store to get some outside toys. They purchase a ball and bat, a soccer ball, and a baby doll. Later, he tells Mina that boys often say things they don't mean. She doesn't understand. "Boys are magnoon (crazy)." He spins his finger to the side of his forehead, and she laughs.

He thinks about when he was a little older than Mina, the day he got beat up at school. His dad sat him down, and he asked Tony about the fight. He was bigger than me, he tearfully told his father. His father, a soldier in the 82nd Airborne, put his hand on his son's shoulder.

"It's not the size of the dog in the fight, it's the size of the fight in the dog." Tony would always remember this. He misses his dad; he had retired shortly after returning from Iraq. His dad always had a persistent cough after he left the military. His dad, already a smoker, spent time in the burning oil fields in Iraq and died during Tony's first year in high school. Tony hoped he could be as good a dad as his father. He would raise Mina to be a winner and put her on a path of success. When they get home, Mina puts on a fashion show, showing off her new clothes. The next day, Mina is wearing the shorts they purchased. The kids thought her prosthetic leg was really cool and were impressed when they saw her move. "Wow, you can run!"

On Saturday, Tony picks up the soccer ball.

"Mina, let's go outside and kick the ball."

She reluctantly goes out, and he kicks the ball to her. She immediately starts crying. Tony realizes the problem.

I'm a bonehead; the last memory of her brother Khalid was kicking the ball and then the explosion. He runs over to her and embraces her, and his mind goes to a dark place, and he starts sobbing.

What if I had gotten there three seconds earlier? They would have both been alive with fewer injuries. What if I had picked up on what was happening sooner? Tony runs through another half dozen scenarios in his head and finally realizes he could not have changed the outcome. What is done is done. After a few minutes they both calm down and go inside. Tony realizes they are both suffering from the trauma. They both need to heal mentally.

The following week, Auntie Kat comes down to visit Mina and help her acclimate to her new surroundings. She brings her a digital tablet.

"She needs this. All the kids have them." Aunt Kat teaches her some simple taps and button functions. Within minutes she is able to use the device like any other kid. Kat takes Mom and Mina to the beauty salon and then to lunch, enjoying a girls' day out.

Chapter Twelve

TONY STRUGGLES TO STAND, his rucksack hanging below his waist. He feels the rush of air as the ramp opens, the light turns green, and the team dives out of the C130. He shuffles down the ramp and dives into the black abyss. He arches hard and gets flat, sees lights in the distance, and follows the team in freefall. As he hits four thousand feet, he pulls the ripcord and follows the other jumpers down. He makes a wide turn, following the pack as they approach the Drop Zone. He dumps air by pulling down the handles, flares, and brakes, and then makes a stand-up landing.

Tony follows the team as they cache their gear, and he follows them through the woodline. He is functioning as an observer controller while the red team breaches a satellite receiving station. Hours later, Tony conducts an after-action review and offers recommendations.

He links up with Mac, Greg, and Tommy, who have been observing other teams on the ground. Mac asks,

"How was the jump?"

"It went well, though not as much fun as they make out on TV."

"Go figure." They laugh.

Tony becomes well known around the community; he is invited to attend some of the astronaut training as a guest and is able to 'hang' with the astronaut candidates. He shows he is comfortable in the Neutral Buoyancy Tank in Houston, Texas. He has performed water operations and is comfortable working in a spacesuit. Despite missing two fingers, he can perform the assigned tasks and manipulate the tools effectively. The other candidates are impressed by his abilities. He gets a chance to participate in high-G training in a centrifuge and is able to pull 7 Gs. He is able to keep up with the best and has made friends in the space program and is invited to come back at a later time.

Over the next several years, the team engages in a number of missions and events; they instruct quick reaction force teams, conduct vulnerability assessments of critical infrastructure, attend training, and function as liaisons to military and commercial space agencies.

Tony continues his education by earning a bachelor's degree followed by a master's degree in engineering sciences, and he also files three different patents for medical devices. As space tourism becomes more mainstream, Tony gets a chance to take a trip aboard a space capsule. Tony is selected to join a small group to travel to the lower regions of space. On board the commercial spacecraft, he is able to experience the sensation of weightlessness for four minutes. He observes Earth from a vantage that few people are able to experience. He feels fortunate his team is able to travel, and they attend various space-related conferences and demonstrations in the US and overseas. He has had the opportunity to visit countries such as Russia, Uzbekistan, France, Italy, Japan, and others that are actively engaged in space exploration and commerce. Space ventures have increased at an accelerated pace since the launch of the Artemis program, and this trend continues until the bottom drops out.

Chapter Thirteen

AT USSPACECOM, THE monitors for space debris turn red. There has been a collision of two satellites. The debris field is approaching the Chinese space station, Tiangong. A call goes out to NASA: "We are tracking a space debris field that is on course to hit the Tiangong Space Station. Can you verify?"

"We see it too; we are sending word to the Chinese Space Agency of an imminent threat to their space station." The liaison officer contacts his Chinese counterpart. Within minutes, the Chinese Space Agency sends a warning signal to the Tiangong. Onboard, the crew has just finished breakfast and will start their assigned duties. Commander Wang has just received the schedule for the next twenty-four hours. Everything is on a tight schedule.

Klaxons start blaring, and red lights go off in all areas. Impact alert. The crew knows this is no drill, and radar senses fragments coming toward the space station at tremendous speed. The pilot checks the controls; he cannot maneuver away. He can only move out of the way to avoid the larger pieces. The crew is silent as large pieces of debris are seen from the portholes. Smaller pieces ping off the hull of the space station. An explosion; the hull is compromised. The gash is big, about thirty centimeters by almost half a meter. The crew loses their balance and is unable to repair the damage. There is no time; air is bleeding off too quickly for the onboard systems to replenish. Wang makes a quick decision; he thinks about his family as he moves toward the breach and puts his back to the gaping hole and mutters his last words.

Immediately blood, bone, and tissue seal the breach, enough for the atmosphere in the space station to stabilize. Soon the cascading debris ceases. The two crew members seal up the bulkhead and notify their command of what happened and the brave act of Commander Wang.

The crew makes a plan and, in the next several hours, conducts an extravehicular activity (EVA) to make repairs on the outside of the hull. When they complete the repairs, they return to carefully remove Commander Wang's body from the breach and finish repairing the inside hull after spacewalking and inspecting the remainder of the hull.

USSPACECOM sets up a screen to determine spacecraft at risk. Starting with the International Space Station (ISS), risk is low for the next 36 hours. The satellite arrays for cell phones and Internet satellite companies have a moderate warning for the next thirty-six hours. USSPACECOM and NASA have sent appropriate notifications to the commercial space companies regarding the risk to other satellite systems.

Seventy-four hours later...

"ISS The debris field is heading your way; additional fragmentation came off the Chinese ISS solar array. We need you to take evasive action in nineteen minutes. We are providing you with the necessary instructions and time to execute the maneuver. The team is headed by Commander Walter Scott.

"We have nineteen minutes to make that maneuver as the crew members hear the transmission."

"Stevens, check to see that the Soyuz capsule is ready for undocking if needed."

"Martinez, make sure the Dragon capsule is ready for undocking as well."

"Mitchell, walk us through the checklist."

"DePalma and Uchenko button up everything that can come loose."

"And Dr. Wu, check on all life support systems and make ready any medical supplies that we might need."

"Curtis, make sure we have equipment on hand for any hull breach and put on your spacesuit." Commander Scott says,

"I'll suit up as well, and may God help us." The crew, already briefed on what happened to the Tiangong, are aware of the risks and hope for the best. The team performs the assigned duties, no chatter, everyone is focused, and tension is high. Stevens informs Scott about the status of the Soyuz capsule. Since Stevens is the pilot, Mitchell calls out to various crew members as he goes through the checklist. Time seems to go slowly, but then the countdown to the thrusters begins. The debris avoidance maneuver involves firing thrusters on the ISS for five minutes and thirty-one seconds; the adjustment raises the ISS orbit to provide crew members avoidance of any debris from the recent collisions. Stevens manipulates the thrusters, initiating the ISS's movement and achieving the desired position flawlessly. After a few minutes, the crew members observe debris flying dangerously close to the ISS. Everyone is holding on; then a violent vibration is felt in the ISS.

"Check systems for damage."

"There is a hull breach by the galley, the port solar array is damaged, and there is a vapor leak, possibly a water line." Mitchell responds. Monitors light up and alarms go off. Scott calls for status. Crew members check the Environmental Control and Life Support System (ECLSS), which manages oxygen. The processes of generation, carbon dioxide removal, water recycling, and temperature regulation are critical; any failure in these systems could directly impact crew safety.

"We are losing pressure on the water system in the ACLS (Advanced Closed Loop System)," Stevens calls out.

Ten minutes later, Curtis gives an update.

"Captain, we sustained some damage to the ROSA (Roll-Out Solar Array) that degraded output by eleven percent. We had a two-centimeter breach of the hull and a leak in the return water line. The leak has been fixed, and the hull has been repaired. We must do an EVA to fix the ROSA struts and inspect the hull for more damage."

They contact NASA Mission Support, advising of the EVA plan.

"Roger, ISS, we estimate six hours to the window to conduct EVA for repairs." Two crew members are assigned to conduct a sweep of all areas of the ISS during daylight conditions to check areas in question. They monitor all feeds to detect any damage or anomalies.

Two areas require physical inspection: Mitchell and Martinez don their EVA suits, proceed with checks, enter the airlock, close the hatch, and depressurize it. They exit the portal and reseal the hatch. The astronauts start to work on the priority repairs, repairing the hull leak and determining if there are any more leaks not picked up by the sensors and cameras. After they check the hull repair, they reinforce it with special adhesive and a patch. They start moving across the main axis toward the damaged ROSA when they start seeing small fragments bounce off the panels.

"More debris is dropping around us. We are moving to the earth side." The astronauts start moving towards the safer area. "I'm hit! My right leg," Martinez communicates. Alarms go off in his suit and on the ISS. Mitchell moves to his location. Martinez is trying to cover the hole with his gloved hand. Mitchell sees a second hole, and blood is vaporizing out of it. He immediately grabs the leg and tries to stop the leak. Pressure is dropping, but he is able to slow down the leak. "We need to get to the airlock." Mitchell has to do this by himself since Martinez is now unconscious. He opens the hatch of the airlock and pushes Martinez into it, and then he enters and pressurizes. After the airlock reaches one atmosphere, crew members pull the injured astronaut inside, pull off his helmet, and administer oxygen via an oxygen tank and Ambu bag to force air into Martinez's lungs. His complexion is bluish gray, and he needs oxygen. The crew members start taking off the EVA suit. Though the wound is small, the astronaut has lost significant blood. They start chest compressions, and the astronaut starts breathing. Still not conscious, he starts writhing in pain. He exhibits bends; the loss of pressure has caused nitrogen to boil in his circulatory system. "Let's get him to the sick bay."

NASA is advised of the accident and reaches out to counterparts from other nations. A decision is made to bring Martinez back with two crew members on board the Soyuz capsule. Due to safety concerns, the remaining crew will use the Dragon capsule if the situation degrades.

Ten hours later, Martinez, DePalma, and Uchenko board the Soyuz capsule. They select Uchenko because he has the most familiarity with the Soyuz. As the Soyuz travels through the atmosphere, the astronauts experience buffeting. Once the capsule travels through the lower regions of the atmosphere, the parachutes deploy, landing on the steppes of Kazakhstan. Martinez is immediately brought to the medical center, where he receives constant attention in the intensive care ward.

Hector Martinez dies three days later.

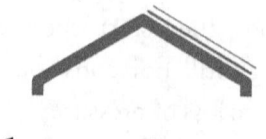

Chapter Fourteen

THEIR SON PICKS THEM up at their modest two-bedroom clapboard house. They eagerly run out of their house with suitcases in their hands. They run through a litany of reminders. Did you take your keys, your wallet, your purse, your passport, the tickets, travel documents...

They sit in the back, ready for the trip to the airport.

"Wow, thanks for driving, Pete. Pretty dismal-looking day out there."

"Yeah, Dad, traffic is crazy today; it's like people have never driven in rain before."

"I'm glad you're driving. I don't have the patience anymore, especially driving on the Long Island Expressway." His wife responds,

"Well, the weather in Europe is supposed to be ideal this week; I can't wait to get there."

"Mom, enjoy the ride. We should get to the airport in about ninety minutes." Pete drops them off at the departing terminal at LaGuardia Airport; they go through the gate, get their boarding passes, and proceed through TSA inspections. Normally, they would be frustrated at the process, but this is a trip of a lifetime. Joe Williams saved up for years for this moment. He and his wife, Serena, have been married for forty years. He has worked in insurance as a senior manager; now, at age sixty-eight, he has just retired. A trip to Paris has been in the plan for the last five years, and now it is going to happen.

They board the plane, get seated comfortably, and are amazed when they break through the heavy cloud cover and see the clear blue skies. They are excited to take this trip and recheck the itinerary for the next few days. They will see the Eiffel Tower, the Louvre, the Moulin Rouge, and a bus tour of sites outside the city. An hour from De Gaulle Airport, the flight attendant makes an announcement.

"The fasten seatbelt light is on. Please return to your seats and fasten your seatbelts. The pilot has detected some turbulence. We will turn off the seatbelt light when the pilot feels it is safe to do so."

Serena asks Joe, "Is this normal?"

"Yes, I have been on many flights where they turn on the seatbelt light; it's just normal air travel."

As he looks out of the right window, he sees something flash by. Then something else rapidly flies by. *Strange.*

A moment later, a baseball-sized hole appears on the wing. The jet violently shakes. *Gunfire? An explosion?* Then something blows off the right engine. As the jet airliner plummets towards the ocean, Joe grabs Serena's hand; they lock eyes, spending their last moments on earth together.

Chapter Fifteen

AN EMERGENCY MEETING is being held at the newly established International Space Agency, which consists of the world's leading space-capable countries and associated organizations focused on space safety and debris monitoring. The agency currently has twenty-seven member countries, with seven additional memberships pending.

Dr Laurence Price, a physicist from the European Space Agency

"Given the recent events of the last few days, we need to quickly find a way to decrease the hazards that are affecting our space vehicles in orbit around the earth. It is now the most dangerous time since manned space flight began. In 2018 it was estimated that two hundred to four hundred tracked objects enter the earth's atmosphere every year. Today it may be twenty to fifty times that number.

According to a document submitted by the FAA, orbital debris, fragmented material from anti-satellite tests, upper-stage explosions, accidental collisions, nonfunctional spacecraft, rocket bodies, and mission-related items have greatly congested low earth orbit and present high hazards to future and current missions, both manned and unmanned. Collisions between objects will eventually become the major source of debris. Due to the high velocity and density of these objects, any collision will cause hundreds to thousands of fragments. The problem is compounded by the Kessler Syndrome, a scenario where the density of space debris reaches a critical point. Collisions become so frequent that they create a cascading effect, generating even more debris and making space travel increasingly hazardous. As the debris field grows denser, the risk of further collisions increases exponentially, rendering certain orbits unusable for future generations. We are quickly approaching that point. Additional collisions are going to occur. This threat could soon escalate dramatically with the deployment of large constellations of small satellites in the already-congested Low Earth Orbit region. Communications satellite constellations will increase the likelihood of collisions. However, since they operate in the lower portion of the low earth orbit, they themselves are more at risk than posing a risk. From the NASA Orbital Debris Program Office, As of January 2022, the amount of material orbiting the Earth exceeded nine thousand metric tons. This number is now significantly higher given the high frequency of satellite launches. It has been well established that the higher the altitude, the longer the orbital debris will typically remain in Earth orbit. Space debris below six hundred kilometers normally falls back to Earth within several years. At altitudes above eight hundred kilometers, the time for orbital decay is often measured in centuries. Above one thousand kilometers, orbital debris will continue to circle around the Earth for a thousand years or more. The fatalities from the ISS, the Chinese space station, and the one hundred and forty-six souls on board the passenger jet en route to France are unacceptable losses and should never have occurred. Therefore, we must impose strict limitations on space travel, allowing it only for reasons related to human safety.

The closing of the International Space Agency Conference:

"We need solutions, and we brought the best minds together from government, science, and industry around the globe to tackle this problem." The chairman pauses.

"In the last few days, problems have been identified, courses of action have been discussed, and solutions have been considered that are reflected in short-, medium-, and long-term planning stages. In the short term, the agreement is to have an immediate moratorium on all space missions for the next six months unless it impacts human safety, resupply to astronauts in low earth orbit, or resupply to those astronauts working on the moon.

The medium solution requires satellites to pass rigorous regulations that guarantee the end of their life cycle, with the safe disposal of satellites ensuring no additional space debris. Altitude restrictions must be adhered to, with minimal deviations to ensure minimal de-orbit and avoidance of populated areas and earth-based travel routes.

Long-term plans include pushing space junk to Very Low Earth Orbit (VLEO) using manned or unmanned spacecraft. Anti-satellite missiles (ASATs), which utilize kinetic missiles instead of explosive-type weapons, would serve as a final option."

Designed in the early part of the Cold War era, all parties agree not to use nuclear weapons.

As the conference winds down, Artemis Sinclair presents an option that has not been considered in the conference. A new technology that shows promise...

"We have a brief presentation, and with your permission, we would like to present it to this assembly," Artemis says. The chairman approves, and then Stilwell joins Artemis to load the presentation together. As they speak to the assembly, people are intrigued by the plan. When they complete the presentation, the chairman asks,

"How long would it take from design time to launch?" Stilwell answers,

"It would take six years; however, we have been working on this problem, and we can launch in six months with approval." This causes a stir. Artemis explains this originally was a response to a Request for Proposal from NASA almost ten years earlier, but funding was halted. Despite the lack of funding and resources, DCI persistently worked on the project. As the conference concludes, major news stations interview Artemis and Stilwell, elevating them to the status of persons of the week.

Chapter Sixteen

AS TONY, MAC, GREG, and Tommy walk into the DC Coliseum, they are amazed by the number of people entering the venue. Judging by the international flavor, it is evident this is a global event. Up until recently, no one took seriously the threat to satellites in near-Earth orbit. Now there is a moratorium on all space flights, manned and unmanned, until a solution can be found to reduce space debris. The risk to space travel has worldwide implications that could threaten monetary systems, communications, and human life. This particular conference would go on for four days, with subsequent breakout sessions likely to follow. The Civic Center was recently updated for this conference and promised to be the most advanced audiovisual experience to date.

"Hey, Bud. You're the last guy I would expect to see here," Nick said with a smile.

"I thought you didn't like dog and pony shows."

"Yeah, I don't, but I heard the food is good," Tony responds.

"Yeah, it is for someone who routinely eats MREs."

"It's great to see you up and walking around again." Nick gives him a 'man-hug,' and they talk about family and how Julie and the kids are doing. Tony tells him how Mina is growing up and adjusting well.

"Well, I've got to get ready to put on a good show."

He leaves with a wave and goes into the auditorium.

The audience for this event consists of scientists, technicians, military personnel, dignitaries, legislators, academics, contractors, and the public at large. Mac and the group interact with many familiar faces, and everyone is swapping digital or physical business cards.

"This thing is going to kick off in about twenty minutes. Let's get some good seats." Mac says.

Unlike other conferences, these briefings are open source, and while there are no concerns about classified briefings or Non-Disclosure Agreements for Intellectual Property, Delphi Combined Industry executives feel confident that their position as the top technology company will not be in jeopardy from competing companies. Like a stage During the production, the light dims and brightens three times, signaling the start of the presentation.

The speaker approaches the podium dressed in a standard gray suit and purple tie. He is tall and lanky in his fifties, no doubt a retired military officer.

"Welcome, I am Nathan Long, Vice President of Space Platforms for Delphi Combined Industries. I am a former Air Force colonel and have been working with Delphi for the past five years. Delphi Combined Industries is the world leader in space exploration and associated technologies. Over the next few days, DCI will present problems and courses of action, and with your help, grade courses of action to find a solution to the most pressing challenge we are facing today."

Tony whispers to Mac,

"Is this where we all get the free coffee mugs and stress balls?"

"Yeah, it sure sounds that way."

For the next ten minutes, Long presents the technological advances of DCI over the last decade, extolling the successes in medicine, conservation, communications, security, digital currency security, energy, and, of course, space systems.

After he presents the speakers for the conference, he introduces Artemis Sinclair, the CEO of Delphi Collective Industries. Artemis greets the crowd.

"Welcome to our event, and I am sure you will enjoy the next few days, and I hope you find this conference worthwhile ... I encourage you to interact with our staff to answer any questions you may have." As Artemis exits the stage, the next speaker approaches the stage: a man with graying hair, balding, and a neatly trimmed beard.

"I am Doctor Evan Marshall with DCI. I work on DCI's Space System team. I have also worked at Jet Propulsion Labs and NASA." He pauses.

"As you have followed the news for the last six weeks, there have been several occurrences that have taken place in low earth orbit, or LEO. There have been countless hours of speeches and testimony presented at the recent newly formed International Space Advisory Committee, who say space travel is now more dangerous since manned flight began. How did we get here? Let's cover the history of space travel. From the early beginnings to today, various events, technological advancements, and mistakes have contributed to this moment. Decades ago, major powers were fixated on the Cold War and the fear of weapons in space. More specifically, satellites equipped with weapons to destroy satellites or targets on Earth. This led to the development of anti-satellite missiles, or ASAT. Various prototypes were designed and built in the sixties and seventies that were explosive, kinetic, and even nuclear.

In 1985, a pilot flew an F-15 to thirty-eight thousand feet and launched a kinetic anti-satellite missile, or ASAT, hitting and destroying a non-responding weather satellite over three hundred miles away in low earth orbit. Over the years there have been other events, intentional and unintentional. The Chinese anti-satellite test targeting China's Fengyun-1C weather satellite created thousands of objects over ten centimeters in size. In 2009, two communication satellites, a commercial satellite phone carrier, and a derelict Russian military Kosmos 2251 accidentally collided at a speed of eleven point seven kilometers per second, or twenty-six thousand miles per hour, at an altitude of four hundred and ninety miles above Siberia. It was the first hypervelocity collision between two satellites. Other incidents involved collisions between satellites and space debris. In 2012, astronauts on board the ISS had to enter the Soyuz capsules when a fragment from a collision passed the ISS, missing it by only three hundred and twenty meters.

In 2021 Russia tested a Direct-Ascent Anti-Satellite missile (DA-ASAT) targeting a Russian KOSMOS 1408 satellite, creating a debris field in low-Earth orbit. The test generated well over fifteen hundred pieces of trackable orbital debris and will likely generate hundreds of thousands of pieces of smaller orbital debris.

The USSPACECOM commander issued this statement. 'Russia has demonstrated a deliberate disregard for the security, safety, stability, and long-term sustainability of the space domain for all nations. Debris created by Russia's DA-ASAT will continue to pose a threat to activities in outer space for years to come, putting satellites and space missions at risk'. The reality is we can only track debris ten centimeters or greater. Please remember that a four-millimeter fragment, which is the size of a BB and traveling at speeds more than fifteen times that of a bullet, can be catastrophic to any spacecraft."

As the day goes on, different speakers touch on the risks of space travel, flight dynamics of certain spacecraft, and definitions of the structure of space.

Nathan Long again approaches the podium.

"Earlier today I said you will have a chance to provide input to the problem of space debris. Let's define the problem statement." Moderators with microphones allow people to make their recommendations, defining the problem statement. Once they finish, the responses are projected onto the large screen. "Now, let's define some courses of action." Again, moderators move around the room, and finally about twelve responses show up on the screen. "Now everyone has a keypad by your seat, and I want you to select from the best to the worst by selecting the numbers that correspond to the solutions you have picked. When everyone finishes, the top three answers are highlighted along with the percentages.

"Now let me show you the results from the International Space Agency."

The results are very similar.

"Now I want to show you the results from the same problem ten years ago with our scientists from DCI."

The results are slightly different but very close.

"Great, you are all thinking like scientists! We will introduce another course of action to the problem statement tomorrow."

The next day is the highlight of the conference. Artemis Sinclair takes the stage to a standing ovation. A giant screen ensures everyone has an unobstructed view. To her left is another podium.

"Good morning, everyone. I am Artemis Sinclair, and I would like you to meet the person you have all been dying to meet." Suddenly, a hologram appears of a beautiful Greek *goddess* with dark hair and an olive complexion dressed in a Greek-fashion, single-shouldered archer dress.

"Good morning, everyone." And then she says good morning in over twenty languages. Foreign delegations are provided with headphones that translate the proceedings.

"And good morning to you, Artemis."

"And good morning to you, Pythia!" The crowd goes wild. They knew this was going to take place, but the visuals were stunning, like a Las Vegas show.

Artemis speaks. "Over the past two days, information has been shared by our Delphi staff and by you as well. Let's start this off with a little practical joke. Some of you have seen this before, but it is always good as an icebreaker." Artemis opens the lid of a potato chip can and lets out a shriek and a laugh as three brightly covered plastic snakes spring out of the can. Pythia mimics Artemis, and the crowd roars with laughter. The jumbotron replays the video in slow motion.

"Now that you have spent the last few days with us, you have undoubtedly reached the same conclusions as we have. You may be asking how we are going to clean up space and recycle the space junk. Snakes in a can!"

The crowd starts murmuring; they are completely baffled.

"I am going to turn the rest of this segment over to Pythia."

"Well hello again, wasn't Artemis great?" She turns and gives Artemis a golf clap.

"Let's zoom in on that video again and slow it down to three frames a second." The audience sees the compressed snakes starting to elongate until they reach their full length. "This is a very simple illustration of the old adage, 'Big things come in small packages.'" She points to the jumbotron to show a low earth orbit simulation. A space vehicle enters the frame, basically a cylindrical rocket. The nose cone pivots away, thrusters slow the vehicle down, and a metallic-covered object emerges, expanding outward and circumferentially to a size many times larger than the cylinder. 'The snake in the can'!" She pauses for the applause.

"The space barge consists of two opposing helical coils and brackets that will lock into place when it fully expands. As the coils intersect, they will be under high tension, and a process called cold welding will occur. The joints will be bonded together due to the pressure exerted by the coils, the low temperature, and the vacuum of space. Cold welding has been problematic in the past and has led to equipment failures in antenna arrays in early satellites. Now it can be used for a useful purpose. Cold welding occurs between two similar metals that are clean and devoid of any oxidation layer. In this case it allows for the rapid construction of the hull. Now, in anticipation of your obvious questions, here is a video taken about eight years ago. A scale model of the helical coils are in the rocket assembly; as in the animation, the nose cone pivots away, releasing three small *snakes* that are preheated. You can see the scale models expanding until they reach their full length. In this experiment, the models were approximately eight feet long. The time-lapse video shows the metal bonding together from a closeup of one of the models. This occurs due to the interaction of atoms between both sets of coils. The electron activity speeds up as the atoms align themselves between two surfaces. Over time, the metal will fuse. The resulting bond will be stronger than conventional welding and will occur quickly. In this next video, the destructive testing showed that the cold weld was over twice as strong as using conventional welds." The animation returns on the screen.

"Covering the hull is a woven metal composite fabric that will hold the shape of the internal framework and form the hull. This metal fabric is similar in appearance to screening used for storm windows in homes. The fabric will stretch around the formed elliptical shape and will also undergo cold welding, forming a semi-rigid hull. The outside of the fabric will be sprayed with a special resin containing carbon nanoparticles; this graphene atmospheric oxygen slurry will be sprayed to the outside of the hull while the vessel is in Very Low Earth Orbit. At this point, two robots, or should I say non-organic crew members, are spraying the barge." She pauses as the participants chuckle at the comment.

"The hull will rotate slowly to promote polymerization from the sun. Rockets will later be attached to the lower deck. Bulkheads and internal decks will be added."

The animation becomes more intricate as pieces are added to the barge. The video culminates in showcasing the completed prototype. Everyone seems awestruck.

"Great job, Pythia! Artemis announces, "Isn't she terrific! Let's go on break before we get into the details." People are eager to ask questions, but Artemis operates according to her schedule.

The next part of the program involves the internal infrastructure of the space barge and includes discussion on landing bays, propulsion systems, and the crew requirements. There are no human crew members, so life support is not needed and greatly simplifies the process. Artemis addresses the audience.

"This concept, developed over ten years ago, was a response to a Request For Proposal from NASA. The original intent was to provide a cargo capability to the Artemis Mission, supporting the Lunar Gateway program involving resources placed in cislunar orbit. The advantages of using cislunar orbit allow for the ability to conduct both missions efficiently. Using low power, the space barge will spiral to higher earth orbit altitudes and at the same time remove space debris. When the space barge reaches the optimum altitude, it will move out of a geosynchronous orbit and transfer to a Cislunar orbit, where gravitational forces from the earth and moon will enable the most fuel-efficient route. The tradeoff: it will take two to three months to reach the moon. Providing supply and resupply to the moon base has always been a concern, as costs per kilo have become too expensive. As low earth orbit became more congested and more dangerous, DCI pivoted to provide multiple solutions and adopted the two-mission approach." Artemis outlines the crew and their duties.

"The crew follows a chain of command similar to naval vessels: the captain, the navigator, the quartermaster, the boatswain, the first mate, the second mate, and the third mate. The Third Mate robot will do simple repetitive tasks. Collecting smaller pieces of space debris. Then sort and place them into designated containers. The second mate will be involved in satellite and stage assembly capture. First mates will be involved in more complex disassembly, removing solar panels, antennas, and probes. The quartermaster will be tasked with securing larger space debris, safely securing potential loose parts, de-energizing live circuits, storing fuels and hydraulics, and organizing the cargo hold. The boatswain maintains the SpaceBarge and performs any necessary repairs to the decks and to the bays. Artemis faces the curtain to the right.

"Here is our captain, who will be responsible for the space barge Argo." A female humanoid robot walks out. About seven feet tall, the robot is exquisite. The robot features a white exoskeleton, a female body with bright blue metallic stripes adorning her human-like arms and legs, large bright blue eyes, and a perpetual smile. The robot displays very real mannerisms, and Artemis says, "Captain, show them what you can do." The robot goes into a handstand, then lowers her legs backward and gracefully stands up. She picks up a massive I-beam that has been placed on the stage over her head, then slowly places it back down without a sound. She then walks over to a table, picks up a piece of paper, folds it into a paper plane in three seconds, and throws the plane, which gently glides towards the audience. The auditorium explodes with applause.

"Thank you, Captain." The robot bows like someone from a Broadway show and then waves as she exits the stage. Artemis has a knack for showmanship and continues her presentation.

Artemis reviews additional duties when the space barge is docked, when it is in orbit around the moon, and when the space barge is traveling between sectors. At this point Artemis again has Pythia continue the presentation and shows a descriptive video of each crew member performing assigned duties and additional tasks. Pythia begins.

"Similar to an ocean barge, the crew fills the interior of the space barge in a pre-programmed manner, separating certain metals and crude disassembly of mechanical and electronic systems. This allows for effective transfer of materials to the moon colonies and will help with the recycling and remanufacturing of needed parts. Metals are broken down into ferrous and nonferrous metals. The intent is to provide materials for manufacturing on the moon. At this time there are several colonies starting on the moon; the Artemis Base Camp is Earth-facing, making it easier for engineers to communicate with astronauts working on the moon. The space barge will deploy two shuttlecraft to provide the delivery of materials to and from the moon. When the space barge returns from the moon, it will dock at the spaceport. Cargo shipped from the moon will be transferred to spacecraft from Earth docked at the spaceport or temporarily stored at the warehousing facility. Each space barge has four landing bays and can accommodate all craft now in existence. The SpacePort will initially look like a large letter 'T.' The top of the T will be where the initial space barge, the Argo, will dock. The two future space barges, which will be considerably longer, will be accommodated on either side of the long axis. The SpacePort will have a three-level substructure allowing for additional modifications and additions, interconnected by a series of gangways, both open and enclosed, to allow the transfer of materials, personnel, and equipment. The substructure will be the first part assembled and will be under tension as it snaps into place. The completed substructure will then undergo cold welding, producing strong bonds allowing for the assembly of decking and the superstructure. With the main or top deck, there will also be infrastructure including a command center, warehouse, and powered launch ramps that will provide a power assist to launch shuttles to various commercial and international space stations. The SpacePort will alleviate the need for 'disposable spacecraft.' The uses of Automated Transfer Vehicles, also known as ATVs, were launched by the European Space Agency to deliver hardware, science experiments, food, fuel, and water for the astronauts aboard the ISS. Once the docked ATV expended all usable items, it would decouple from the ISS and enter and burn up in Earth's atmosphere. The HII Transfer Vehicle, also known as HTV, was another disposable spacecraft used to resupply the ISS. With the erection of the SpacePort, this would preclude the use of expendable craft. The onsite warehouse would allow for a small fleet of automated shuttles to provide the delivery of supplies to and from the space stations. When not in use, the shuttles would be docked at the spaceport. Any waste from the space stations could be loaded on low-tech containers at the spaceport and jettisoned back through Earth's atmosphere via the powered launch ramps and burn up upon re-entry. The construction of the SpacePort will precede the assembly of the Space Barges. We will repair, update, and improve space barges based on mission dictates and transshipment demands as the program matures. When the initial space barge is completed and conducts a successful mission, another space barge will be assembled. As the mission progresses, there will be additional barges brought online as the need or demand arises. SpaceBarges will dock at the SpacePort to refuel and transfer supplies to and from the moon. We will limit space to twenty-five percent of the payload volume; this is to free up room for the primary mission of collection of space debris and subsequent voyage to the lunar gateway for unloading. As the primary mission starts to wind down with the collection of space debris, activities on the moon will increase. This will include water resourcing, fuel and oxygen generation, and manufacturing of facilities and needed equipment. If successful, the SpaceBarge program will be expanded to missions to Mars and beyond.

Thank you all for your attention."

"Thank you, Pyria." Artemis gives a final wave, and the hologram fades out. Applause lasts minutes. Artemis signals to hold the applause.

"At this time we will take questions; I or my staff will answer."

"Will Pythia be back?" Someone yells.

"I'm still here," she answers. The audience laughs.

"Yes, she is still here and will be called on to answer questions that I or the staff may need help with." Additional questions are taken from a podium set up in the middle aisle.

"Hi, I'm Thomas Willis from Space Systems LLC.

"Will there be any human crew members on board in future iterations?"

"Not at this time; it may be eventually. We don't rule out another life-supporting craft accompanying the barges for scientific study, but we have not worked on any life-supporting system built specifically into the barge itself." Artemis looks back to the panel to see if anyone has any further input. "Well, thank you, Thomas, for that question." Eugene Johnson from Space Systems asks,

"What are the command, control, communications, and computer requirements?"

"Dr. Leonard, our chief scientist, can provide the best answer."

"Excellent question," Dr. Leonard comments. "Command and control of the space barge will be performed via quantum teleportation between Pythia and the onboard quantum computer. Communications will be instantaneous, and it will be the first mission to use this technology. This use of quantum teleportation involves quantum entanglement between Pythia and the onboard quantum computer system. This will provide a communication link, enabling the transmission of instructions from Pythia and monitoring of systems from the onboard computer. Pythia will provide constant feedback to NASA, USSPACECOM, and DCI, along with other strategic partners. Dr Leonard asks,

"Pythia, can you display a graphic showing quantum teleportation?"

A simple graphic appears on the screen showing an arrow with labels. The first label represents 'Incoming Photon,' the second label represents 'Entangled Photon Pair,' and the final label, 'Teleported Photon.' The graphic also shows dotted lines indicating a quantum channel alongside dotted lines showing a classical communication channel. Dr. Leonard provides a comprehensive presentation about quantum entanglement and the other communication systems on board the space barge.

The next question comes from Dr. Ethan Brooks, from NASA.

"Is the expandable hull design scalable?"

Nick is called on to answer the question.

"That is a good question; the design is indeed scalable. The design allows for a hull to be either smaller or larger. In fact, the plans call for a later-generation hull to double in length and triple in volume."

The next few people introduce themselves and ask simple questions, resulting in simple answers and further buy-in from the audience.

Although Mac does not like the idea, Tony wants to ask a question. Tony gets up and introduces himself as Anthony Demarco from the US Space Force.

"What does Delphi Combined Industries get out of this since you will be the exclusive carrier of materials to and from the earth and the moon?" Artemis smiles and says,

"I think Pythia can provide you with the best answer."

Here are the Big Guns, Tony muses.

To his amazement, Pythia appears on her podium.

"Well hello, Master Sergeant Demarco, Thank you for your service." She starts to clap as well as everyone in the auditorium.

"Master Sergeant DeMarco is a highly decorated Special Forces soldier now assigned to the US Space Force. Welcome."

Tony is blushing; Pythia apparently knows everyone in this auditorium by facial recognition and can tap into their bio. *This is unnerving.*

"To answer your question, may I call you Anthony?"

"My friends call me Tony."

"Oh, we're friends now. Great! OK, Tony." She smiles, and the audience laughs.

"To answer your question adequately, I prepared this presentation." Up on the screen a 2D animation appears. It shows representations of the space barges and a large circle that says Earth and a smaller circle showing the moon.

"You can see the percentage of payload space change by monthly increments. Cargo originating from Earth is green, space junk is shown in red, and goods from the moon are yellow. In seven years, the primary mission will end, and subsequent missions involving the exploration of Mars will ensue. As to the integration of other companies, there will be a lot of work for everyone." She pauses, and the audience claps.

"Similar to ocean barges, the space barges will need logistical support in loading, unloading, and transfer to and from earthbound spacecraft. Long-haul shipping by rail, ship, truck, or plane, as well as last-mile deliveries and warehousing, will require additional support on earth. The list goes on. Delphi Combined Industries is about innovation; change brings new opportunities, and we are eager to work with our partners in this undertaking. As far as costs, they will be less than half the cost per kilo of goods now for delivery to the moon, including all ancillary costs. Over time these costs could go down significantly. Thank you, Tony, for that question."

"Thank you, Pythia," and again Artemis takes over the questions as Pythia fades from sight. Tony returns to sit next to Mac.

"Did you get her number, hotshot? She seems to like you." Tony couldn't help but laugh. He recalled the old W. C. Fields quote that his father had taught him.

"If you can't dazzle them with your brilliance, baffle them with your bullshit."

Only he did not know if this was brilliance.

Chapter Seventeen

THE SPACEPORT WAS SIMILAR in design to the space barge in that it was a prefabricated assembly expanding out of the cylindrical container. Once out, a girder assembly unrolled with cross bracing locking into place. Six assemblies were needed to complete the main structure. Once the main structure was completed, the support systems were erected over the next several weeks. Another six assemblies were constructed to build out the superstructure, gangways, and conveyance equipment. It only took forty-nine days to complete the spaceport, able to accommodate three SpaceBarges and landing pads for spacecraft. In addition to the landing pads and docking capabilities, the SpacePort provides warehousing for materials waiting to ship or to be picked up from the moon. The spaceport also has RP-1 rocket fuel, oxygen compounds, and other propellants and can provide refueling capabilities to several different spacecraft. The powered launch system utilizes induction propulsion capable of launching objects in any direction. The SpacePort is maneuvered to a higher altitude, and all systems are in place by day seventy-nine.

The first space barge assembly launches ten days later and enters a low earth orbit. The compressed hull takes twenty-nine hours to stretch out to three hundred meters as the inner coils unwind and it fully expands the metal fabric. Internal gussets are attached to the intersecting coils, and bulkheads and decks are added to the vessel. Once the internal hardware, decks, and bulkheads are completed, the carbon nanofiber slurry is applied to the outer hull. The hull rotates, and the sun hardens the surface, making a surface stronger than tungsten steel but more flexible and less brittle. This initial space barge is half the length of the intended final model and has one-third of the volume. The next stages involve completing the lower deck and cargo hold area along with the command and control module mounted by the quarterdeck in the aft section. Overall, it takes only forty-seven days to complete the construction of the first barge. It is christened with the name Argo. It takes an additional fifty-six hours to complete all system checks. The first mission will be to enter the highest density debris field located in the six hundred and eighty to eight hundred and twenty kilometer range. Debris ranging in size from thirty to one hundred and fifty centimeters will be the first space junk collected. Also collected will be pieces smaller than twenty centimeters in a basket-type container carried by the Third Mate robots that will orbit the Argo. As the work progresses, near real-time reports are sent to USSPACECOM and NASA, who will send rollup reports to the International Space Agency. Within eight weeks, the first shipment of space junk is headed toward the lunar gateway. The Argo makes its way to lunar orbit, deploying a landing shuttle to the lunar surface. Contents delivered in special bags are lowered to the lunar surface without the shuttle having to land. The other shuttle launches and deliveries of cargo are done in a similar manner. The operation progresses smoothly. Later iterations include the downloading of space debris and the uploading of materials from the moon. The operation lasts eleven hours and marks a success at the halfway point. The Argo completes its mission and returns to the spaceport. Material from the moon is transferred to shuttles standing by at the spaceport. The shuttle's crew has temporarily stored shipments slated for the moon in the warehousing structure adjacent to the dock. The transfer of cargo and materials to shuttles would proceed more quickly in subsequent missions. The next launch tests the ability of the Argo and the crew to capture a large piece of space junk. The intended target is the core stage of a Chinese Long March 5B rocket. The rocket with the fuel expended is at risk of re-entering the atmosphere in an uncontrolled manner. A similar March 5B rocket stage had crashed into two villages on the Ivory Coast, destroying buildings, but fortunately, with no loss of life. The Argo crew successfully disassembles and stores the derelict rocket stage. Within nine months the full-size design of the SpaceBarge was completed with three times the volume of the Argo. The SpaceBarge, Paralos, has a total length of six hundred meters and a diameter of twenty meters. To test the capability, the Paralos attempts to capture an environmental satellite, one of the most advanced and largest Earth observation satellites ever built. Operated by the European Space Agency (ESA), it was designed to monitor and study Earth's environment, including its atmosphere, oceans, land, and ice. The satellite contributed significantly to environmental science and exceeded its planned five-year mission, operating for ten years. Despite efforts, the ESA lost contact with the satellite and could not restore communication. At over eight metric tons and an altitude of eight hundred kilometers in low earth orbit, the satellite remains a threat to future space missions. This is the first mission to try to retrieve and disassemble a large-sized derelict satellite. The robotic crew successfully contains and removes the solar arrays, storing them in the interior of the cavernous space barge. The derelict satellite is towed to the rear deck and drained of propellants and hazardous waste. The satellite is loaded in one piece, proving Paralos capable of capturing and storing large-scale space debris. Salaminia, the third vessel in the fleet, joins them eight months later. The operation continues smoothly, and DCI is right on track with forecasts. Over the next three years, forty percent of the space debris is eliminated from lower Earth orbit. Shipments to and from the moon are also increasing in frequency, and the moon is quickly being colonized.

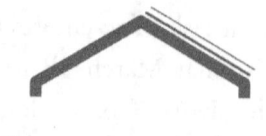

Chapter Eighteen

AT TEN THIRTY IN THE evening, Mina comes home from the dance. Tony says,

"How was the dance?"

"It was OK, nothing special. Hey Dad, I'm sorry about before; I was just freaking out. I didn't want to be late; Marsha's mom took us and picked us up at ten."

"That's OK, Mina. You may not believe this, but I was a teenager at one time." She laughs, "You are still a teenager." Tony laughs as well.

"Are you ready for your retirement ceremony?"

"Yes and no. It's really not a retirement, just a transition into civilian life. You can't really live on military retirement pay the way you would like in today's economy."

"So what are you going to do?"

"I will be doing pretty much the same type of work; only as a contractor, I'll be working for Uncle Mac at his company."

Mac retired as a 'Full Bird' Colonel about two years prior and had set up a contracting company with transitioning personnel from Special Ops, calling the company Daedalus Group. With government and civilian space businesses, there was always plenty of work in security, analytics, engineering, testing, and other support work. Tony could work on different contracts that required certain skills. He could work as much or as little as he wanted. He had established a solid reputation and amassed a substantial savings account thanks to Nick's investment advice. Contracting work also pays substantially more than the military. It was a bittersweet moment. On one hand, you are transitioning from one career to another, yet you consistently find yourself reflecting on your past accomplishments. You think back to the relationships that fade over time. Mom had flown to Virginia and would come back with Uncle Bill and Aunt Mary to attend his retirement ceremony. Greg would also be retiring. Both of them will be retiring as sergeant major, avoiding the more mundane duties associated with that rank. Tommy retired as a master sergeant the year before, and he was Mac's go-to guy. Still physically fit, he possessed a sharp wit and a positive attitude. For the past six months, he would call Tony about twice a month.

"Tony, when are you going to stop playing soldier and get a real job?"

Over time, Mina turned into a bright, athletic teenager who could do anything she put her mind to. They were good together and would pull strength from each other. Tony was as strong as he was ten years ago, maybe even better. He maintained the discipline that he had on an A team but was able to hit the gym more often than when he was on long deployments. Mina excelled at many sports and was not held back by any handicap. Whether playing basketball or performing ballet, she could function at a high level. Tony taught her to throw a football, and they would toss the ball around every so often. With Tony's engineering skills, he designed high-performance prosthetics that allowed Mina and others to compete at the highest level. Mina was slated to go to the Paralympic tryouts in a couple of years, and Tony couldn't be prouder. He could not have raised her without the help of his mother. Mom would keep her centered and help her navigate through the rough patches, with the help of Auntie Kat, whom Mina called frequently. Tony continued to advance his engineering skills and developed a state-of-the-art sports glove. The glove allowed the prosthetic fingers to open and close as he moved his middle finger, enabling him to play football, basketball, and baseball. He enjoys life while still doing the things he loves, but now he has to embrace the next chapter of life. His retirement ceremony marks one of his happiest memories, surrounded by many friends and the people he loves.

"Hey Tony, are you still riding?" Uncle Bill says.

"Yep, but mostly just to and from the base. I heard you got a new set of wheels."

"Yeah, I got demoted down to a trike by your Aunt Mary. She was worried."

"That's still cool. What did you get?"

"A reverse trike, two wheels in the front—Aunt Mary even rides with me sometimes."

"Great, enjoy it." Then Tony hears a familiar voice.

"Hi Tony, How are you?"

"Great, how are you, Doctor Suarez?"

"I'm still Gabe to you. I'm better than I deserve; I finished my residency, and I will be a flight surgeon at NASA next month. I have to thank you for your recommendation; it went a long way in helping me get into NASA."

"Well, if it weren't for you, I may not have been here; you saved my life."

"Doctor Gabe," Mina yells. "Thank you for coming. I wasn't sure you could make it."

"I can't miss a chance to see my favorite patient."

Mina gives him a big hug and tells him about her life, ambitions, and accomplishments. Tony just smiles; he is proud of how Mina adapted to a new life.

"Hey, stranger, how is it going?" Nick says.

"Great, I see you brought the crew. Hi, Julie. Wow, the kids are getting big. Mina walks over. "Uncle Nick, Aunt Julie, how are you?"

"We are doing great," Nick says.

"Mina, how are you doing?"

"Really good. I just love Rosie. Thank you, she is an enormous help."

"Rosie?" Nick looks at Tony.

"The robot you gave us. She named it Rosie."

"Like the Jetsons. Cool, enjoy it." Nick says. Tony engages in conversations with everyone, concluding the evening with the thought,

It's been a good run; it's time to turn the page.

He's ready to start a new life and take things a little easier.

Chapter Nineteen

SIX MONTHS LATER, ALMOST biblical in nature, a technological plague occurs in various parts of the world. Innocuous at first, it does not become a major concern. Phone carriers from North America, Europe, and Asia start experiencing call drops, and towers seem to be working sporadically. All efforts to make repairs find that there is nothing wrong with the systems, and after several hours, they seem to work normally. Several hours later, emergency call centers are experiencing disruptions affecting people's safety in cities around the world. Texting becomes haphazard, and except for short texts, "text not delivered" becomes a common message. The next day, the top credit card systems start to act sporadically, and a third of all transactions fail. People believe that ransomware is affecting the systems, but after eight hours, no cyber group has responded to claim responsibility. Stores and businesses start to take cash only. After three days, all credit card transactions were halted. Countries suspect state-sponsored economic terrorism and try to take actions to find the source. Arrival and departure boards at transportation hubs show a 'blue screen of death,' not showing the incoming and outgoing transportation assets in India, Iran, and Pakistan, leaving passengers stranded or not departing on schedule. Banks run out of physical currency since people are starting to make a run on the banks. In the US, the sixteenth-largest bank loses a significant amount of deposits in a short period of time. The bank's stock price immediately plummets by sixty-eight percent. In China, the Industrial and Commercial Bank, the largest asset lender, experiences disruptions of certain systems but does not divulge the exact losses. At a rural bank in China, authorities violently disperse a peaceful protest by hundreds of depositors, who seek in vain to demand their life savings back from the bank. At the European Central Bank, protests turn violent as thousands clash with police in the German financial capital in response to misinformation spreading through social media. Conspiracy theories are amassing from all around the world, leading to frequent and bloody confrontations. A rash of AI news stories starts hitting the Internet, not 'fake news' taking things out of context or stories that are heavily biased, but 'deep fakes' where the content is completely fabricated and seems to have the appearance and voices of trusted journalists. No one seems to research and check the veracity of the videos people are adding to social media. Instead, people are perpetuating myths by not checking the authenticity of the videos they are posting. This sparks riots and violence around the globe, as people share these false 'stories' across all social media platforms. Crowds begin attacking businesses falsely blamed for high prices. The AI-generated false representations of respected and trusted journalists have caused unrest and mistrust of all governments and institutions. Crime has increased in major cities and has spread worldwide. There is a rise in the number of suicides due to the despair bombarding social media.

Leaders do their best to try to calm the masses, but it has little to no effect. People believe what they want to believe and start hitting the streets—looting and maiming people for no discernible reason. Supervisory Control and Data Acquisition systems (SCADA) start getting compromised.

At a Saudi petroleum refinery, Aramco, Mohammed Ahmed has just finished his second back-to-back shift. Production has increased due to the uncertain times. As foreman, Mohammed checks the areas after his crew leaves in preparation for the next crew. While conducting checks, he sees an analog pressure gauge with a needle bouncing between low and high readings. He goes up to the gauge and taps the case, hoping it is just stuck. A moment later he realizes the problem, but it is too late. The valve blows out, killing him instantly, causing a series of intense fires, halting all production. The explosions have taken the lives of twelve workers, injuring twenty-three others. The cyberattacks are believed to be planned by Houthi rebels and carried out by Iranian hackers. This results in attacks on Yemen, starting with the assault on Aden airport.

In Great Britain, a series of thirteen natural gas explosions occur when the aged pipes are over-pressured in Birmingham. Fire departments respond to one hundred and thirty-five fires.

In the US, Colonial Pipeline, a major US fuel distributor, suffers a cyberattack, shutting down pipeline operations and causing fuel shortages along the east coast. A six hundred-foot freighter navigating through Tampa suddenly shears off a support to the Sunshine Skyway Bridge, dropping off a fourteen hundred-foot section of roadway. The accident occurs during rush hour and causes seven vehicles to drop into the water, including a school bus, killing twenty-five people. The ship's radar inexplicably fails minutes before the collision, causing the accident. Other similar incidents happen in Argentina, where a large cargo ship collides with the bridges crossing the Prana River due to a sudden failure of the navigation systems. The bridge remains intact with no loss of life. Five people die in China when a cargo ship's navigational controls fail, causing the ship to ram into a bridge in southern China, cutting the structure in half. No one is claiming responsibility for the cyberattacks. Tension mounts.

Chapter Twenty

NICK TRIES TO CALL Tony; it has been a while. He needs Tony to meet him somewhere.

"Tony, give me a call; it is important. Maybe we can meet somewhere and discuss some things." Things have been tense at work. Over the last year, things have become weird with the company, and the only person he could confide in is his co-worker, Raj Patel. Raj has noticed a change in the climate at work, but he does not understand the severity of the problem. Nick and Raj are kept out of the modifications to the space barges and are given busywork in the form of data analysis of metrics that serve no discernible purpose.

Nick becomes aware of something insidious: modifications to the space barges that make no sense. The space barges are now equipped with a reinforced nose cone assembly and a thicker hull by adding more and more layers of the carbon nanofiber slurry. Office talk has become caustic. Rather than talk about the weather or sports, workers are extolling the virtues of Artificial General Intelligence and how governments are holding mankind back from advancing as a species.

Nick attempts to inform people, but he has to do this undercover with no electronic signature. He had typed warnings out on a thirty-five-year-old computer not connected to the Internet with a direct-wired printer. He circulates the fliers at several libraries fifty miles away with the hopes someone will be able to put this on social media and have federal authorities investigate DCI. His writings, limited in scope and designed to avoid arousing suspicion, are met with silence. Any social media posts label the writings as a conspiracy theory or the ravings of a lunatic.

His supervisor urges Nick to stay after work longer; he has rarely worked this late. He agrees, not really wanting to, but to further avoid suspicion. Nick leaves the office; it's been a long day. He gets into his EV and heads toward home. As he drives, music comes on very loud, and he tries to turn down the volume.

I smell gas. He tries to pull the car over, and the car starts accelerating at a high speed. He keeps hitting the brakes, but no response. He listens to music, an old rock song he has heard before with the words "...the end of the world."

They are on to me. Nick's last thoughts are of his family as his car flips at one hundred and forty miles an hour and bursts into flames.

Chapter Twenty One

THE FBI ARRIVES AT DCI headquarters and asks to see Dr. Artemis Sinclair. Escorted by her assistant, they enter her office and show their badges. "Dr. Sinclair, you are coming with us; you are under arrest," and they read Artemis her Miranda rights.

"Are you mad? Is this some kind of joke?"

"It's no joke. You have created several shell businesses. You have been funneling funds through these companies to offshore accounts. We have tracked over thirty-eight billion dollars of assets."

"I can't believe this. This is a mistake. Can I make a call?" She says, "Pythia, do you know anything about offshore accounts?"

No response. "Pythia? Pythia?" *There is something really wrong.*

As the FBI agents come out with Artemis in handcuffs, the major media companies have set up cameras. There is a team of thirty people in windbreakers with FBI stencils on the back. The lead agent tells the team leader, "Have your people shut down all computers, take statements from all of the employees, and take out physical files and lock up the building." All entrances are taped, further denying entry to every building on campus.

Artemis' attorney later arrives at the FBI field office. Emily Townsend, a woman in her late fifties, has served as the company attorney for twenty years, representing the Sinclair family on numerous occasions and Artemis in several employee disputes that typically settle out of court. She asks,

"Artemis, are you alright? What happened?"

"I don't know. They said I have offshore accounts. I have never done anything illegal with taxes or tried to hide money. I have no idea what is going on."

"The FBI usually won't raid a business unless they have conclusive evidence; somebody could be setting you up. Have you had any conflicts with anyone who might be high in the organization?"

"No," Artemis answers.

"How about in your past, have you had any conflicts?"

"Some, but just petty stuff, years before I became a CEO."

"OK, we will have to hire a private investigator. I have one in mind that only does high-visibility cases, and he has a vetted staff and a proven network." They meet with the FBI, and Attorney Townsend looks at the charges. It takes another day before all the paperwork is submitted, and Artemis is freed after posting bail and surrendering her passport. The judge asks her if there is anything else. Artemis glares at the FBI.

"Why did you shut down, Pythia? It has a critical mission."

"Dr. Sinclair, we don't know what you are talking about. Other than a few mainframes and an older server room, there is no quantum computer in there. We have not shut down any of your systems. Where is your other lab located?"

"There isn't another lab." She is stunned. *What is happening?*

After a few days, the private investigator checks out the lab. No one seemed to have worked there in a while. "Ms. Sinclair, how many times have you gone to the lab?" The private investigator asks.

"I don't know about four times."

"How long were those visits?"

"About twenty minutes—why?"

"I don't think there was a working lab for some time. When was the last time you were there?"

"I saw the equipment. It was three months ago."

"I think what you saw was a ruse. The equipment you saw most likely didn't work or wasn't a quantum computer."

If that was the case, where was Pythia?

Artemis starts making calls. She tries calling the chief operating officer, Adam Burke, who took over after John Stilwell left two years ago. No response. She calls an emergency meeting at a local hotel with everyone in an executive position who is willing to talk to her. *Is Pythia still with us? Who is running the barges?*

Including Artemis, there were only four people. Sheila Thomas, Dr. Lowell Grunwald, and Dr. Rochelle Jackson. The board members are unaware of anything happening. Sheila Thomas, Human Resource Officer, comments,

"There had been an unusually high number of resignations in the recent months."

"Why is that unusual?" Artemis asks.

"No one asks for references or severance pay, and they opt out of extending their health care."

"Sheila, do you have any current employees that still work in the computer lab?"

"I will check; give me a few minutes." When she returns,

"That's strange; every one of them had resigned between two and six months ago. I was never notified." The meeting adjourns with more questions than answers.

"I am going to contact NASA. We have no idea who is controlling the space barges, if anyone. If you hear from any of our employees who may know about the situation, please stay in touch."

Artemis reaches out to Dr. Steven Gillespie, a director at NASA Goddard, and requests a meeting at his location in Maryland. She has two of the board members join her, Doctors Grunwald and Jackson.

She meets with NASA officials, Colonel Morris Mitchell from the US Space Force, and other stakeholders in the space debris program. The basic questions are

Where are the space barges located?

Where are they going, and is Pythia still in control? Artemis conveys the findings from the private investigator that the computer lab seemed like it was a setup, and it was uncertain whether it really housed the quantum computer that held Pythia. The meeting ends quickly, but everyone remains focused on finding answers. Dr. Gillespie from NASA suggests reconvening in two hours and submitting graphics.

Everyone is ready to present their findings. Dr. Gillespie begins.

"The way we are going to do this is one at a time. Colonel Mitchell, can you start this off?"

"Since four days ago, there had been a decrease in communications by Pythia regarding the space barges. As of sixty-six hours ago, we were unable to query her responses. As of this morning, the only information is position and acceleration. At this time the space barges seem to be moving in a controlled manner. This indicates command and control is still operational, but the limited communication from Pythia is concerning." The next up is an analyst from NASA.

"Something is still controlling the space barges and may still be performing the primary mission, but in the past several hours Paralos has increased its altitude by about thirty-eight kilometers. While not unusual, we need to track the position of any of the space barges and report any changes in orbit."

"Dr. Sinclair, do you have any updates?"

"No change. DCI employees have been advised to not enter into conversations with anyone since the FBI raided the offices."

The next stakeholder is a professor of quantum mechanics from MIT. He asks a single question.

"Could it be possible that Pythia has become self-aware and is making decisions for itself? For years, this machine has been treated more like a person than a machine."

"Is that even possible?" Colonel Mitchell asks.

"Given the past makeup, number of qubits, and specifications, probably not if that was the prototype that we saw about three years ago. But not knowing where the lab is located, the machine could have advanced a hundredfold or even a thousandfold, so it could very easily be in the realm of possibility."

"So we just need to shut it down." One of the other attendees speaks up. Dr. Grunwald answers, "It's not that simple. First, we don't know where it is located. Second, we don't know if we could shut it down, even if we knew where it was, since there is no signature."

"What about power consumption? We could track high-energy users."

"Only if they are on the grid. They may be using a solar farm or small modular reactor."

The attendees develop more questions that do not produce any answers, and the meeting becomes counterproductive.

After an hour, Dr Gillespie announces,

"I'm going to send this information to the other agencies. Ms. Sinclair, can you be here at 9:00 am tomorrow?"

"I don't think I have much of a choice."

"In the interim, can you try to reach employees who left the company a few years ago? Maybe they have some additional insights." Her head is spinning; this situation has her rattled, and she doubts her ability to make good decisions. Colonel Mitchell also asks if she could provide the location of the lab and how to enter. She has to confess that the private investigator entered but did not divulge how he did it.

"He might have done it surreptitiously, but I can give you the address."

"Understood. I'll contact the Attorney General's office to make an exception so we can send a team of specialists to verify the findings. They may be able to glean some useful information. This has been elevated to a national security issue."

After a few minutes, the meeting adjourns, and Artemis is ready to leave. Colonel Mitchell asks her if she could meet him in the hall. Artemis cringes but agrees to talk to him. She thinks he is going to admonish her but decides to hear what he has to say.

"I'm sorry for what happened there today, and I know you're between a rock and a hard spot. You need someone to help you through this. I probably shouldn't be telling you this, but you need help outside of the government, someone who can cut the red tape."

"I have an attorney," she says.

"That approach won't help you influence the power players. You need someone who can make things happen."

"You mean like a lobbyist?"

"Not quite. This person has quite a reputation on the Hill, and she can provide the help you need, and she owes me a favor or several favors." He discreetly hands her a business card with a scan code: Katherine DeMarco, Corporate Attorney.

"She's not cheap, but she will get the wheels moving quickly."

"Thanks." Artemis responds.

"Don't thank me. I work for the government, so the next few weeks may be challenging, and unfortunately, I won't be able to assist you."

As she leaves, she feels a little better; at least there are currently people working with her, but there's no telling how long that support will last. When she arrives home, she takes Colonel Mitchell's advice and calls Katherine Demarco.

"Ms. Demarco?"

"Call me Kat. I thought I might hear from you. A friend informed me about your situation, which is not surprising since you have been featured on every news channel lately. How can I help you?"

"I believe I was set up; the company is locked up, I'm facing federal charges, and the space debris project is potentially unsafe."

"OK, let's meet informally, say in about two hours in a public place; we can grab dinner. I'm sure you haven't eaten. There is a small restaurant in Alexandria with only a few patrons, and it will not attract the paparazzi. They serve delicious gyros and shawarma. I'm sure you will enjoy the food. I will meet you there."

The two women meet in the restaurant and introduce themselves. Kat builds rapport talking about simple things like traffic, weather, and the Washington Commanders since she reviewed the bio on Artemis and was struck by her football career in college. This serves as an icebreaker, and Kat compliments her on her athletic goals.

"That was a long time ago," and Artemis laughs. They order dinner and keep the conversation light. After dinner, they order some coffee and begin their business.

"Kat, how can you help me?"

"Well, generally speaking, I'm a persuasive person that can get problems in front of the right people. I saw the news and read many of the articles written about you. Some are not very flattering, but I'm not here to judge. It sounds to me like you were set up as the fall guy, or in this case, the 'fall girl.' We will need to get in contact with some of the people from DCI."

"But they were instructed not to talk to me or anyone from corporate."

"Oh, did I say talk? I meant leverage. If they won't talk to you, we will use other tactics; people often don't know how to keep secrets." Artemis feels better about the conversation.

"My services are a thousand dollars an hour; this meeting is no cost. I know that all your assets have been frozen, so essentially you have no money. If I can't free your assets, you owe me nothing."

"Thank you." Artemis is feeling better.

"Send a list of employees to me, and I will text you tomorrow afternoon. Tell me how it goes and get a good night's rest. We will get things moving; this is going to be a challenge."

When Artemis gets home, she remembers what Colonel Mitchell had said and decides to call her old mentor; she hadn't talked to him since he left DCI over two years ago to retire. She finds his contact info and tries the number. The phone does not ring. She tries his email, and it comes back as 'not a valid email address.' She finds a person's search app and pays the fee. The search comes back with an unknown residence. She thinks he might be outside the country. She calls Emily to see if the private investigator could track down John Stilwell. Two hours later, the attorney calls her back. This guy is a ghost; there is zero paper on him, no trace of him whatsoever. LexisNexis has no hits on him in the past fourteen months. Artemis thinks back to a quote attributed to Sun Tzu, "Never trust a friend who is silent." Artemis realizes she wasn't being mentored; she was being groomed to take a fall. She throws back half a bottle of wine and calls it a night.

As she drifts off to sleep, she thinks,

I trusted you, Uncle John. What did you get me into?

The next day at NASA Goddard, more attendees arrive, prompting the setup of another large room. Representatives from every three-letter and four-letter agency seem to be in attendance. A large number of defense agencies are attending via telepresence and are shown on a large screen. Again, Dr. Gillespie from NASA Goddard moderates the meeting. The meeting starts with introductions and organizations. Artemis has met many of the people attending, and off-site attendees also introduce themselves. To her surprise, Katherine Demarco introduces herself, and the moderator prefaces that Ms. DeMarco has been requested to attend. The federal government invited Demarco to observe and assist as a facilitator. Once the meeting begins, it does not take long for it to devolve and start with finger-pointing. Katherine takes control.

"What we need to do is identify the scope of the problem. Time is short; let's limit questions and responses to two minutes. Please."

The attendees start asking questions.

"What happens if we cut off communications?"

"What happens if we shoot an anti-satellite missile, or ASAT?"

"What if we cut power to the quantum computer?"

Most of the questions are handled by Artemis, Dr. Grunwald, or Dr. Jackson from DCI. Artemis has to endure the barbs and arrows, but she does not let her feelings show. She keeps her stoicism throughout the rest of the day.

Katherine is able to guide the meeting along, at least to build consensus and develop working groups. The next meeting will take place in three days, and there is much to prepare. Through an agreement with the DOJ, Artemis would be allowed to use a satellite office in Pentagon City to access files that she needs.

When Kat comes home, her cell phone rings. "Kat"

"Tony, what's wrong?"

"Nick is dead. They're calling it suicide."

"Oh, Tony, I'm so sorry."

Chapter Twenty Two

TONY ARRIVES AT PHOENIX Airport the next day, rents a car, and goes to Nick's house. He is welcomed with a hug from Julie.

"I'm so sorry, Julie; Nick was the best."

"Tony, he loved you like a brother." He closes his eyes, trying to hold back tears.

"Can you speak at the funeral?"

"I would be honored," Tony says. Julie grabs Tony's hand and talks to him behind closed doors.

"Tony, something's wrong. They said Nick committed suicide. They said he had gambling debts over two hundred and sixty thousand dollars, and he was going to be let go for drinking on the job." Tony feels his temper rising.

"That's B.S. I will take care of this." Tony knew that this was crap; Nick was murdered.

"Julie, we will talk after the funeral." Tony did not want to divulge anything in front of Nick's family. Tony did not discuss this with anyone. For one thing, Nick never gambled. He had visited casinos on two occasions with Tony but would just check out the shops and get something to eat. Nick did not drink and would end up being the designated driver when Tony threw back a couple or more beers. In reality, Nick had been extremely wealthy for years. He followed the markets and made considerable money. Years earlier he told Tony to buy Bitcoin. Bitcoin was under two hundred dollars a coin. Tony bought five coins; Nick bought twenty-five. Neither of them cashed out, so there was serious money. A memorial service is held at the funeral parlor, and Nick's remains are cremated, and his ashes are interred at the nearby cemetery. Nick's brother takes care of the arrangements. At the cemetery, there is a short graveside ceremony, and Tony delivers a eulogy, recounting all the good times they had together and what a true friend he had been to himself and others.

Julie asks Tony to meet her at the house before friends and family arrive for the final gathering. When Tony arrives, Julie opens the door and leads Tony into the study.

"Nick told me to give this to you alone." A heavily taped envelope with the words "For Tony DeMarco Only." Julie hands Tony a knife, and he opens the package.

"I will give you some privacy," Julie says.

"Tony, if you are opening this, it means I didn't make it. There is a cult that is working inside DCI... Their motive is world domination. They intend to destroy major cities, causing a global event. The plan is to disrupt Supervisory Control and Data Acquisition, or SCADA, systems, causing technological disasters. They will probably attack financial systems and weaponize the SpaceBarges. Look up "Rods of God." As Tony reads, he would have just dismissed this as a conspiracy theory, but it was Nick who did not act unless he had factual information. Nick included drawings and formulas to back up his assertions. Nick describes a secret lab that he estimates was up to four hours away but has no exact location. Tony has to let someone know. He let Julie know that something suspicious is going on with DCI, and he needs to do some digging. He calls the best person he knows for this situation.

"Kat, listen I just received some details about Nick. I am sending you a file. Use our internal." Tony has set up a password that only he and Kat know. Tony uses his phone to take pictures of the pertinent papers. He stores the pictures in a password-protected compressed document file and then sends that file to Kat via email.

Kat responds back within fifteen minutes.

"How fast can you get to DC?"

Tony takes the red-eye from Arizona and arrives at Reagan Airport in the early morning.

"How was the flight?"

"Been on worse."

"I'll bet you have. I set up an appointment at the DOJ; they have to see this. You are probably not going to like this, but I took on Artemis Sinclair as a client."

"You what? Are you kidding me!"

"No, it looks like she has been set up, probably by the prior chief operating officer. I don't know what's going on, but I don't think Artemis knows anything about this. She will be attending the meeting."

"Are you sure?" Tony says.

"Well, I told her that the DOJ may be able to release some of her assets if she attends."

"Do you think they are going to do that?"

"No, but this is a national security threat, and we have to lay the cards out on the table."

"Have they seen the file?"

"Yes, I sent it by a trusted courier. I wanted them to see it first since it has personal protected information. I did not want it to go through any other agency that might classify it. It could take weeks before we could get the ball moving."

They arrive at the Department of Justice, an imposing building with strong Art Deco influences. They are escorted upstairs to the conference room. In attendance are the Attorney General, National Security Advisor, Federal Aviation Administration Director, FBI Director, NASA officials, USSPACECOM Director, and, of course, Artemis and her attorney. The Attorney General addresses everyone in the room.

"Before we start, I want you to read the folder in front of you. Dr. Sinclair and Ms. Townsend, you will also have a folder. After you read this, you may confer with your lawyer. We will start the meeting in 30 minutes. Before we start, our security manager will give you a briefing." The briefing is the standard.

"Do not share information about anything in this meeting since it contains highly sensitive information." After Artemis and her lawyer read the information, they go into an adjacent office to talk about the documents.

"Do not answer anything unless you want to respond. Before you answer, look to me, and I will let you know if you can answer. Remember you were Mirandaized just a few days ago."

Artemis and her lawyer take their seats, and the Attorney General initiates, "Good, looks like we have everybody; we can start." Artemis stares at Kat, probably thinking she was thrown to the wolves, which she was.

"Dr. Sinclair, what can you tell us about one of your employees, Dr. Nicholas Siegel?" Artemis looks to her lawyer, and she nods yes.

"Dr. Siegel was a gifted scientist who worked on the space barges, rapidly expanding their internal hull design. He was credited with coining the term snakes in a can,' which we emphasized during our conferences. I had met him only twice, but I knew him more by reputation. I was saddened to learn that he had committed suicide and was heavily in debt, based on the information I received. We sent out our condolences, and we were in the process of reviewing insurance and 401k benefits along with pay for the rest of the month. When the FBI came into my office, all of this had ceased."

"Can you tell me when you first received word of his death?"

"I was contacted the morning after he died by our human resource officer."

"Up to that point, had you heard any derogatory statements about Dr. Siegel?"

"No, as far as that goes, he always did well on annual reviews."

"Can you speculate as to why someone might want to kill Dr. Siegel?"

"My client is not answering that." Attorney Townsend responds.

"Can she tell us the last time she had contact with Pythia?"

"All right, she can respond again because she already responded to that two days ago."

"The day before the FBI came to my office, in the afternoon. I had Pythia answer some rudimentary questions about DCI events scheduled for the next month, and she provided a list. However, the next morning, when the FBI entered my office, Pythia did not respond at all.

"I understand you found out the computer lab was not in use."

Colonel Mitchell from the US Space Force answers.

"I can shed light on that. Ms. Sinclair had someone check the computer lab, and they found it to be essentially empty. The investigator who first examined the lab believed it was a ruse rather than an operational lab. We had our specialists check it out and determined that it had once been a lab with a possible earlier version of a quantum hybrid computer, but now it is essentially empty."

"Do you have any idea where this computer is located?" Artemis whispers to her attorney. Townsend responds,

"She has no idea and cannot speculate."

"Dr. Sinclair, can you look at the note given to Anthony DeMarco where it says a secret lab may be up to four hours from Mesa, Arizona?" Again she defers to her attorney.

"Ms. Sinclair is not aware of any assets other than the research building in Mesa. The chief operating officer would know."

"Where is the Chief Operating Officer?" Artemis responds,

"I have not been able to contact Adam Burke; he doesn't answer any calls, texts, or emails."

"Do you trust him?"

"My client won't answer that question."

"Are you familiar with a cult named Delphi Collective or the Collective?"

"No, I have never heard of a cult by the name of Delphi Collective or Collective."

"Do you think there is a conspiracy?"

"I don't know!" Artemis answers, overcome by the chain of events. The Attorney General asks the FBI Director to comment on the Delphi Collective.

"Until recently, the Delphi Collective, or just Collective, had not been on anyone's radar. They claim they want to save the world from man's destruction of the planet. They claim to be altruistic and that a sentient being would be benevolent and show the way to salvation. They believe that through quantum computing, this being will evolve and fix the world's problems. They classify themselves as a religion and hold 501(c)(3) tax-exempt status. In the past, they have raised billions of dollars. Since the investigation opened regarding the cult Delphi Collective, there have been at least three people who died under suspicious circumstances shortly after they criticized the group. These included Dr. Amy Sharp, a professor at Berkeley who taught computer ethics and apparently fell off a cliff while hiking in Sedona. Dr. Aaron Singer, a noted physicist, died two months ago after allegedly falling off a cruise ship in the Caribbean, with no witnesses. He had written an article published in the Journal of Responsible Computing, citing that the Collective's ideology was based on faulty assumptions. A third person died at a train crossing when her car apparently lost power and the warning lights and drop arm were not functioning. It is still under investigation by the National Transportation Safety Board. She apparently belonged to the group but had misgivings. Some things popped up on the Dark Web where she was voicing her opinion; her name was Evelyn Summers, and she worked in the DCI Mesa Office three years ago. Did you know her?"

"I am not familiar with the name." Townsend interrupts,

"My client has been under a huge amount of stress. What you have shown us today is new to her as it is to you. You need to verify your sources before you accuse my client of anything." There was a silent pause.

"May I?" Tony says, "I am the closest thing to a source you have." Tony briefs the members in the room on the last two days and his relationship with Nick.

"I have been around the block a few times, so I know about handling sources."

"We understand and appreciate your actions. Can you corroborate this with anyone else?"

"I can tell you Nick did not drink, and as far as debt, Nick was probably richer than anyone in this room with the exception of Dr. Sinclair."

"Can you show proof?" The Attorney General asks.

"This is a personal letter to me that was included with the documents; I can show it if need be. Nick entrusted me with his brokerage account. I can show you the current value."

"That would be good." The Attorney General asks the FBI Director to send someone over from Financial Crimes.

"Yes, and I will have someone send leads to the Phoenix Field office. Dr. Sinclair, can you provide us with an employee list from the Mesa office?"

"My client will need access to the office and the computers."

"Agreed, we will make that happen," the attorney general responds.

The meeting turns to the subject of the space barges. "Are they operating independently, or is someone or something controlling them?" Artemis looks at her lawyer. Townsend responds, "We currently do not have an answer, but we hope to find one soon."

Colonel Morris speaks up, saying, "A more precise question might be whether Phythia is still actively controlled with human oversight or if she has full autonomous control and has become self-aware." The Attorney General turns toward Artemis.

"Well, Ms. Sinclair, you have a lot on your plate. Agents will contact you shortly and get you back to your office." He dismisses Dr. Sinclair and Attorney Townsend. They leave without acknowledging Tony or Kat. After they leave, the Attorney General explains, "As some of you probably have guessed, these documents were heavily edited." The Attorney General has someone bring in the other copies.

"According to this, Dr. Siegel noticed that modifications were made to the space barges he had not seen. Why would he think the addition of a nose cone would signify a weaponization of a space barge?"

"Sir, I can answer that," Dr Felix Hansen from DARPA explains "Dr. Siegel mentions 'Rods of God.' The rods of God were a kinetic-type weapon that transitioned from bunker busters in World War II. These munitions were a two-and-a-half-ton weapon that would reach speeds approaching one thousand miles an hour and would take out concrete-reinforced bunkers. During the Gulf War, similar types of kinetic weapons were dropped without rocket assist. DoD engineers created kinetic weapons that could be delivered by a bomber and penetrate eighty feet of concrete. Later, a theory was kicked around about using tungsten steel rods from space, theorizing this could cause damage similar to a tactical nuclear bomb, hence the name 'Rods of God.' The Chinese also tested their version; the results were not as theorized, and the damage was far less than expected. So research stopped. The problem with the weapons is that the trajectory would change due to atmospheric drag and gravity, lowering the effects. According to Dr. Siegel, the space barge hull was reinforced five times thicker with improved carbon coatings and a highly designed nose cone capable of resisting high temperatures of re-entry. The space barges were never meant to return to Earth, so there is no way to land the massive vessels on Earth. The end of the cycle for the space barges was to land on the moon by disassembling or landing with auxiliary rockets in one piece. Due to the low gravity of the moon and lightweight construction, the space barge could land on the moon and serve as warehousing for future operations and further development of the moon. The issue is that if the vessel were filled with enough tonnage, the impact could be catastrophic, affecting not only a single city but also surrounding areas. The resulting damage could be world-changing, not only from the impact but also from the possible changes to the atmosphere and to the ocean if the impact involved coastal targets."

The Attorney General asks,

"What would the effects be on human life?"

"Casualties could be in the tens of thousands to over a million from such an event and the aftermath, but that is just a guess at this point, less maybe if it hits a desert area. The best thing we could do is model a simulation and run scenarios. Either way, it could be a global changing event." The National Security advisor asks,

"What would be the best way to prevent this from happening?"

"The obvious answer would be to disable the command and control or shut down the computer." The National Security Advisor remarks,

"According to Dr. Siegel, the search area could be thousands of square miles. Is there any way we can detect any electronic, heat, or visual signature to find where this lab may be located?" General Miles from Joint Chiefs responds,

"We will coordinate with the other agencies to see if there is something in the inventory that can pick up a signature from a lab of this type." The FBI Director responds,

"I'm authorizing a team of forensics personnel to go out to Mesa to start setting up a Mobile Command Center. The Phoenix office is sending a team to Mesa to check on employees in the area. We have people monitoring the Dark Web to see if we can find any hits on the terms 'Collective' or 'Delphi Collective.'"

The National Security Advisor asks. "What if we cannot find the lab? Is there another way to disable the space barges?" Dr. Hansen from DARPA answers.

"Possibly, but it comes with a lot of risks and possible conflicts with other nations. We could try to shoot a missile to intercept the barge and take out the electronics. It would be a small target that is heavily shielded; it's something we would have to run in simulations." Colonel Mitchell responds,

"We continuously monitor the space barges. As of this morning, the barges are still performing the primary function of collecting space debris." The Attorney General comments, "Since this discussion is moving away from the criminal aspect, we need to shift to a different venue." All agree to reconvene in the Pentagon for follow-on meetings and coordinate with NASA Goddard on the change of venue.

The Attorney General signals Tony and Kat to come into his office. I want to thank you for coming forward with this information. He sets them up in an office so Tony can open Nick's brokerage account. After a few minutes, they verify the total. With the new evidence, a murder investigation is opened. Again they stop by the Attorney General's office, and he welcomes them inside. Kat initiates the conversation.

"Regarding Dr. Sinclair, she has been forthright regarding this matter. I think she can be helpful."

Artemis' phone rings.

"Ms. Sinclair, this is Agent Simmons. I have instructions from the FBI Director to let you into your corporate office so you could provide us with a list of employees from your Mesa office."

"That's correct," Artemis confirms.

"I will meet you in front of your office in one hour."

Artemis meets the agent, and they enter the building. She powers up her computer and is able to access the employee files. She hands a printed list to Simmons.

"Thanks, you can stay in the office, and you can start bringing your employees back." An hour later, the Attorney General calls.

"Dr. Sinclair, I called up to explain that since portions of the meeting had gone beyond the scope of a criminal investigation, they were not germane to the case. Since the case has reverted to a national security matter, you will be contacted for the upcoming meetings where you will receive full disclosure."

"Thank you, I appreciate that." Artemis responds.

"Dr. Sinclair, you may want to reach out to Katherine DeMarco; she definitely has your back." As she hangs up, she thinks,

I guess I was wrong; she isn't a backstabbing bitch.

Chapter Twenty Three

CYBERATTACKS ESCALATE and hit major infrastructure systems. Rail systems in North America, Europe, and Asia are heavily automated and are being targeted. Warning systems, including lights and audible signals and drop arms at railroad crossings, stop working, resulting in a high number of accidents. Railroad switches are not functioning correctly, and the track indicator lights are malfunctioning, affecting passenger, freight, and commuter trains. A higher incidence of derailments has been occurring. Accidents turn more deadly with tanker cars rupturing and spilling volatile or toxic compounds. In Ohio there is an accident that causes the derailment of fifty-three cars. The toxic compounds seep into the groundwater, and the air quality is deemed unsafe, prompting officials to declare a state of emergency, calling residents to shelter in place.

In Italy, a train switch 'fails,' causing a passenger train to derail. The train operating at a speed of 300 kilometers per hour is sent down a section of track only rated at sixty-two kilometers per hour. Twelve people are killed and thirty-eight injured.

Hundreds of passengers had to be evacuated after a high-speed intercity express train in Germany struck a truck that was driving through a train crossing, killing eight people, including three children under the age of five. Numerous others sustained injuries.

Dozens of people are hurt when a train strikes a fire engine in Florida. Train warning signals not operating leads to more accidents at train crossings during the evening hours.

There is an escalation in violence and looting in almost every major city.

At major airports, a series of computer shutdowns affects air safety by shutting down systems for air traffic control. The shutdowns only last for several minutes; they confound information technology personnel who are unable to find the cause. The nature of the threat has yet to be determined; most accidents occur on the runways. At London Heathrow and Chicago Midway airports, there have been two near collisions, but they were avoided by the actions of the air crews.

Looting has changed; people are not breaking into high-end stores but are stealing from grocery, hardware, and convenience stores. Pharmacies are broken into by people looking to score controlled narcotics and other pain remedies.

The Internet is running more false stories, fueling the passions of extremist groups on both sides of the political spectrum. People are literally killing each other to get the meager supplies of gasoline and diesel fuel.

Teenagers are openly carrying weapons, itching to play out their fantasies from video games, trying to imitate soldiers from elite units. People have been going to churches to find solace and peace from what is happening around them.

Cities have cut off electricity to try to quell the mobs, and some cities have declared martial law. Instead of offering assistance during attacks on individuals, onlookers use their cell phones to record footage. The few rational individuals who attempt to dissuade the mobs often face defeat.

Doomsday prophets are also out predicting the end of the world with signs saying, Repent. Across the globe, most cities are enforcing curfews that have resulted in the deaths of those disregarding the warnings.

The countries with nuclear weapons have started initial staging. Warheads are being prepared and mounted. Russia and China have prepared missiles aimed at US targets. Israel has nuclear weapons aimed at past aggressors in the Middle East. India and Pakistan have rekindled past animosities and have ramped up their systems against each other. North Korea has targets selected in Western Europe and US territories. The US, Great Britain, and France have ramped up missile defense capabilities to protect NATO alliances and other countries that may be at risk. Iran has weapons staged, but it is unknown what capability they have.

The world is on the brink of thermonuclear war.

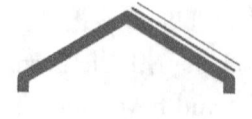

Chapter Twenty Four

AT USSPACECOM, THE overnight shift detects a rapid change in the speed and altitude of the space barge Paralos. It has started to go into the higher reaches of low earth orbit. NASA is contacted to confirm the position. The commander comes in and asks for updates. "Sir, the Paralos is still gaining altitude." "Does anyone have an idea where it might be heading?"

"We have some ideas, but they are not definitive; we can try to run it through Apollo." Apollo is the name of the SpaceCom quantum computer.

"We could have Apollo check the course of possible space junk or satellites it might be targeting,"

"It's worth a try," the officer in charge responds. The next hour, the team puts together all the information they think is pertinent. The team generates a report with the results in a few minutes. The satellites that the team identifies have a probability of eleven to thirty-four percent. The probable location is Middle Earth Orbit with a probability of seventy-one percent but with the caveat 'more information required.'

"What does that mean?" Someone asks. The officer in charge answers. "We have a lot of work to do. Update the report in fifteen-minute increments to see if Apollo provides more specific information. Run additional queries if you can refine the parameters."

Two hours later, Apollo narrows down the prediction. US Global Positioning System satellites and Chinese and Japanese Global

Positioning System satellites are at risk. A call is made to the White House. "We have a problem. The space barge, Paralos, is entering into Middle Earth Orbit, and navigation satellites from China, Japan, and the US have been identified." An alert is sent to the White House, Department of State (DOS), Joint Chiefs of Staff (JCS), National Security Agency (NSA), Defense Advanced Research Projects Agency (DARPA), Department of Defense Agencies, Federal Aviation Administration (FAA), Department of Transportation (DOT), and Missile Defense Agency (MDA). The space agencies of China and Japan have been notified about the potential targeting of their satellite systems. They set up a timetable, anticipating a potential attack within the next three hours. The president calls together the national security advisor and representation from the Pentagon and sends a car with Secret Service agents to bring in Artemis Sinclair and board member Dr. Lowell Grunwald. The FBI shows up at her door. "Dr. Sinclair, you need to come with us."

"Am I under arrest?"

"No, ma'am, the President needs you to come to the White House. Dr. Sinclair, please dress as quickly as possible. This is a national security issue."

"Do I need my lawyer?" "No, ma'am, it's not about your case. Another team is bringing your colleague, Dr. Lowell Grunwald."

As the SpaceBarge Paralos starts moving into Middle Earth Orbit, USSPACECOM reports,

"SpaceBarge Paralos has disabled and captured a Chinese global positioning satellite." Frantic calls are made around the world; continuous reports are sent to all stakeholders. The president opens a dialogue with the Chinese chairman:

"We are trying to get control of the SpaceBarge Paralos at this time." The chairman responds.

"You must get this space barge under control. We have set up anti-satellite missiles as we speak. We will shoot at this space barge unless the United States does something to stop this."

The Chinese are notified that there is a high probability that another satellite may be captured in four hours. USSPACECOM monitors the launch of Direct Ascent Anti-Satellite (DA-ASAT) from a Jin-class nuclear submarine in the South China Sea. The DA-ASAT is headed toward Paralos. As the missile starts to come within range of the Paralos, it veers off, unable to hit the target. A half hour later, the submarine launches another DA-ASAT. From USSPACECOM, the monitor picks up the trajectory of the missile, and it is on course. When it starts getting in range of the Paralos, again the missile veers wide of its target. Two half hours later, the Paralos disables and captures a second Chinese satellite.

Artemis is escorted into the White House, where all the decision-makers have assembled and talks have already begun.

"Dr. Sinclair, please take a seat. I am sorry for the short notice, but the SpaceBarge Paralos has already attacked two Chinese global positioning satellites. The chairman has already launched several anti-satellite missiles to destroy the SpaceBarge. Both missiles failed to reach the target." At this point, DCI's board member and assistant technology officer, Dr. Lowell Grunwald, is being led inside. As he sits down and Artemis asks him directly,

"What will happen if an ASAT hits the space barge?"

"If it hits, it may sustain some damage. In theory, if it hits the command module, it may disable the space barge. I want to emphasize that my remarks are conditional, starting with the word 'if.' The Paralos is equipped with an active multi-sensor system and a mechanism to disable missile guidance systems. The Paralos is also equipped with a high-energy burst system and a high-energy laser as part of its defense systems."

"So are you saying we can't physically stop the Paralos?" The president asks.

"No, what I am saying is that it would be extremely hard."

"Can we shut down the computer? Can we stop Pythia?"

"Mr. President," he turns to face Artemis, "we have not been able to locate the computer." The NASA director intervenes.

"Sir, in the meetings we had at Goddard, Dr. Sinclair advised us that the computer that now hosts Pythia is believed to be operating in the desert somewhere in Arizona."

"Now what do we do?" The president asks. "We have been sending aircraft over the area, and we are prioritizing satellite coverage over Arizona. We have not been able to detect any possible location for the computer."

The president excuses himself and confers with several of his advisors. They all agree that the US should show good faith and are working on a solution. The phone call is short. The president divulges the existence of active security systems on the SpaceBarge, and the chairman says only two words:

"I understand," and the call ends.

Later, USSPACECOM monitors yet another launch of DA-ASAT from a Jin-class nuclear submarine in the South China Sea. The missiles are on course to intercept the Paralos, then veer off, out of range, unable to hit the Paralos. Soon, the Paralos intercepts, captures, and de-energizes another Chinese navigation satellite. Within the hour, two self-driving heavy cargo trucks veer off the road in Southern China. At least sixteen people have died in the two accidents in southern China, according to Reuters and other international news outlets. Other collisions occur, causing a fifty-kilometer traffic jam on the Beijing-Tibet Expressway. The president tries to make a call to the chairman, but the Chinese refuse to take the call. USSPACECOM detects a launch of three more DA-ASATs from the Jin-class submarine. An urgent telephone call is patched through to the Situation Room.

"Mr. President, the Chinese have launched three more anti-satellite missiles, but not at the Paralos. We believe they are on course to take out our GPS satellites."

The president informs the staff. A helpless feeling is shared by everyone in the room. They quickly decide to send an alert advising all users not to use self-driving or attempt to use GPS-assisted systems. As they begin taking steps, USSPACECOM mirrors the live feed of the radar to the Situation Room. Two of the satellites in the GPS constellation are destroyed. Later a third satellite is destroyed. US news stations start reporting numerous crashes occurring across the United States, Canada, and Mexico. The space war has begun. The Commander-in-Chief exclaims.

"We need a solution to this problem! Dr. Sinclair, what resources do you have at your disposal?"

"Sir, I was arrested this week and had my assets frozen. I only have limited access to my company, and my employees have been locked out." Within twenty minutes, an executive action is initiated under the Defense Production Act. DCI is open again for business.

"Ms. Sinclair, get your best people at a meeting in your headquarters; I will send our audio-visual specialist to set up a secure line for teleconference." Artemis reaches out to Dr. Rochelle Jackson to arrange a meeting room at DCI headquarters, letting her know that DCI is operational and ensuring she has the necessary staff for the meeting. Artemis calls Human Resource Officer Sheila Thomas to arrange to have the top DCI scientists come in to attend the teleconference.

Several hours later, the president again contacts China, questioning the provocative action that they took.

"This is unacceptable; this was a totally unreasonable action." The chairman says, "If one of our satellites is attacked, we will destroy two of yours." The President urges,

"You have to understand this is not the US; this is a terrorist group that has taken control of a commercial spacecraft. The Chairman responds,

"I have to protect my country any way I can; I cannot help it if you have lost control." The president is furious but does not want to escalate the situation.

"I will meet with my advisors to come to a solution."

"I hope you do." The chairman ends the call.

Chapter Twenty Five

USSPACECOM DETECTS the Paralos has changed course.

"Sir, I have movement on the Paralos; it looks like it has started to gain altitude."

"Roger, give us updates every fifteen minutes." A query is typed for Apollo to track a possible destination. The result is a ninety percent probability that the next target may be the Russian Global Navigation Satellite System (GLONASS) in five and a half hours. Again, the White House is advised of the situation. Communications are set up with the Russian president. "...the attacks are not from the US; there is a terrorist organization known as the Delphi Collective. They have taken control of the commercial space barges. These assets have cleared space debris and have greatly assisted space ventures for all space countries, including Russia and its allies. The United States and Russia have had longstanding partnerships for many decades. We are asking you to maintain restraint while we try to develop a viable solution. Members of your own space agency, Roscosmos, are assisting us with the planning." After a pause, the Russian president answers.

"We have no choice but to disable your space barge before it inflicts further damage. It is in our best interest."

"But it won't work. Anti-satellite missiles have been ineffective."

"We have the capability; we will make it work." The call ends. The President goes back into the meeting and asks the NASA Director to reach out to his counterpart to appeal to the Russian President. The NASA director speaks to his counterpart, but his appeal fails. Russia intends to use an explosive anti-satellite missile or, worse, a nuclear warhead that could destroy nearly all electronic systems in space and cause outages to Earth-based communications systems.

With the Paralos causing havoc in space, no anti-satellite missiles have been able to disable the craft. The Paralos, equipped with large-scale jamming capabilities, disabled communications and guidance systems; current unmanned space vehicles could not be used due to the risk of loss of guidance systems, leaving few options. It became clear that stopping the Paralos would require the use of a manned spacecraft.

A special meeting is called at US Space Force regarding the existence of a new space vehicle with weapons capability.

"Can anyone tell me about the 37B?" Someone responds,

"It is an uncrewed mini space shuttle used for military and scientific tests. It has conducted long-term flights for three years or longer."

"Is anyone familiar with the 37C?" A hand goes up.

"It was a rumor that a 37B could be modified for a manned flight shuttle, but it was just a theoretical paper."

"It's no longer a theory; it has been tested and has flown several missions. The important thing to understand is that, unlike other manned spacecraft, the 37C can fly completely on manual control and can be launched on an Atlas rocket. Due to the nature of the mission, the space barge Paralos has several security countermeasures that have diverted potential strikes from anti-satellite missiles. This mission is unique; it will be the first manned mission involved in direct action to take out a spacecraft from space. As we speak, we have a team working on the engagement strategies and weapon systems that can be utilized.

We have very few specifics on the countermeasure technologies onboard the Paralos. Needless to say, this will be a high-risk mission."

The next part of the discussion addresses the capabilities, specifications, avionics, and flight dynamics of the 37C. The NASA astronaut program pairs a trained Space Force Guardian with a NASA astronaut in preparation for the mission. Another team has been designated as an alternate, and the teams start planning directly following the meeting. The other attendees are tasked with providing updates and any information that will help with training or provide needed insights for the mission.

After two hours, it is imminent that SpaceBarge will capture the Russian GLONASS satellite. The Russians have two new Direct Ascent Anti-Satellite missiles, or DA-ASATs, ready for launch. In the Situation Room, Dr. Gillespie from Nasa explains,

"...The fear is the unknown of whether the DA-ASATs carry a nuclear warhead. A space-initiated blast would be minimal, unlike nuclear weapons tested in the atmosphere that created a large, distinctive mushroom cloud and destroyed objects with high pressure. However, the effects could be devastating, destroying almost every satellite in the line of sight. EMP releases electrons by utilizing high-energy gamma rays from a nuclear explosion, which interact with air molecules in the upper atmosphere, causing them to ionize and release electrons, known as Compton electrons, that are then propelled by the Earth's magnetic field, generating a powerful electromagnetic pulse across a wide area. During the late 1950s to the early 1960s, the United States carried out several high-altitude nuclear detonations, including the 1.4-megaton Starfish Prime test that occurred two hundred and fifty miles above the Pacific Ocean. The Starfish Prime nuclear test explosion produced radiation belts that lingered for months, disabling eight of the twenty-four satellites that were in orbit at that time. Since we have no visibility on a potential Russian nuclear warhead, we don't know what the overall effects would be, only that it would cause irreparable damage to systems worldwide."

As USSPACECOM is monitoring a potential launch, it sends the latest update.

"Signal Intelligence has detected activity at the Plesetsk Cosmodrome in Northern Russia. After a few minutes, "Confirmed launch of one DA-ASAT." A second DA-ASAT launches two minutes later. Space Command is monitoring a countdown clock that indicates the time remaining until the target is reached. The feed is also viewed in the White House Situation Room. As the clock runs down, everyone is looking at the monitor, waiting for the signature showing an explosion. The time-to-target clock runs down, and the clock is adding seconds. +1...+2...+3

The clock goes on for several minutes. USSPACECOM issues a statement: "We have an explosion high above satellite range." A few minutes later, they detect the second explosion. The SECDEF is online and receives a briefing of what occurred. The Officer in charge responds,

"The missiles deviated away from the Paralos, missing it, and they kept going further out into space. The Russians initiated a self-destruct command. The DA-ASATs did not have nuclear capability." A collective sigh is heard across the room.

As warned, the Paralos captures the Russian GLONASS satellite. Two hours later, Russia finds another GLONASS satellite is at risk. Communications are made directly with USSPACECOM, who confirms the information. Russia indicates they will take additional defensive measures.

Again, USSPACECOM monitors the launch of a third and then a fourth DA-ASAT on course to disable or destroy the Paralos. Everyone is watching the screen as the time-to-target reaches zero and begins to count up: +1...+2...+3. USSPACECOM issues an update: "DA-ASATs three and four from Plesetsk Cosmodrome deviated away from the target, and a self-destruct command was issued. No nuclear capability detected." Once more, anxious tension subsides with a sense of relief. Within two hours, Paralos captures and deenergizes the satellite. Russia connects with the White House. The Russian president lashes out, "This is unacceptable; you have failed to solve the problem! Any US spacecraft launching from the United States will be shot down. We have equipped a rocket with a nuclear warhead. We will find a way to deal with this threat."

The major news channels report, Attempt to Destroy Space Barge Unsuccessful." In a related story, DCI has been reopened, and the employees can return to work. The media assumes the space barges are yet another technology that has been hacked by the rash of cyber terrorists. In a show of solidarity, China issued a similar ultimatum.

"Any spacecraft launching from the continental US or any of the US territories will be destroyed."

Chapter Twenty Six

IN THE PHOENIX FIELD Office of the FBI, a caller urgently wants to talk to an agent regarding Delphi Combined Industries; he has information regarding the suicide of Dr. Nicholas Siegel, but he needs protection. An agent working on the case picks up the phone. "This is Special Agent Jake Collins. How can I help you?"

"Sir, My name is Rajesh Patel. I worked with Nick Siegel. I have to talk to you, but it is not safe for me and my family. I am calling you from a burner phone. I am afraid they are tracking me." "Who are they?" Jake asks. "The Collective," he responds. A nondescript work van picks Rajesh up from a vacant area and brings him to the safe house. Rajesh is sweating.

"Can you protect me and my family?"

"Probably. Let's see what you know first."

The FBI agents do not want to waste time on someone who does not have actionable intelligence. They run a profile on Rajesh and know that he has worked with Nick Siegel on the same project for the past four years. Rajesh opens up

"I have known Nick since we started working for DCI, and we worked very well together. On the first space barge, the Argo, we were heavily involved in planning the hull design. We designed the internal expanding structure that formed the hull and the locking mechanisms as well as the metal fabric covering. Things were going well for the first three years, but later, strange things started happening. In the design of the two full-sized barges, we were not allowed to work on the modifications that were made to the hull design, and we were approached several times by senior executives acting very strange and just making unusual small talk." Jake asks,

"What kind of small talk?" "Things were innocuous at first, like, 'Many historians believe that most of the wars were started because of religion.'" Another time, they argued that we wouldn't have all of our current problems if the world united as a single planet rather than as separate countries.

"Why do you think Nick was murdered?" Agent Collins asks.

"Nick was pretty vocal. In addition to being pissed off with the secret work modifying the space barges, he found out that a nose cone was made for the Argo. The Argo was Nick's baby; he came up with the internal structure, hull, and all external features."

"I don't see a connection; why is a nose cone a problem?"

"The nose cone is made of a tungsten carbide frame with twelve high-temperature laminate/ceramic-carbon tiles."

"Why is that so important?" The agent asks.

"The only reason the barges would need a nose cone would be to enter Earth's atmosphere, in other words, to crash into Earth."

Rajesh spends the next hour divulging all he knows about possible members of the Collective. He believes Stilwell is probably part of the hierarchy of the Collective; he had left the company two years ago but may still have influence in the organization. After he reveals all he knows, Rajesh asks about witness protection. Jake says, "We are taking your family to a safehouse, but I'm afraid you have to come with us."

"Am I being arrested?" Rajesh nervously asks.

"No, but you are in custody. We are taking you to Washington. For your protection, we are going to say you are under arrest. We want as many law enforcement people around to protect you. We will be leaving for the airport in an hour. Relax; the FBI director wants to speak to you directly." The FBI instructs Rajesh to call home using his burner phone; he feels anxious and doesn't know what to say. He is in tears and tells his wife not to worry, but she and their daughter have to go with Special Agent Anita Sanchez. Special Agent Collins monitors the pickup of Rajesh Patel's family, ensuring their safety.

The FBI agents escort Patel through the airport terminal along with air marshals, local law enforcement, and airport police. They board the flight with no issues and arrive at Reagan Airport, again with an entourage of agents and law enforcement personnel escorting them to the waiting FBI bureau car. The handcuffs are taken off once they enter the car, and Patel watches as they travel up 14th Street. Patel is shocked when the car turns into 1600 Pennsylvania Avenue and enters the White House gates. The group is met and brought into an office.

"Dr. Patel, my agents have told me you have been very cooperative. That's encouraging; we need your assistance to manage this situation effectively. Dr. Patel, since you are now involved, I will ask Special Agent Collins to tell you what we know."

"The group who allegedly killed Dr. Siegel has been around for a few years and was known simply as Delphi, since many of the original members worked for DCI. Several years ago they merged with another faction called the Collective and became known as the Delphi Collective. What is important is that, up to this point, Delphi were highly educated scientists and engineers. They formed a cult that deified AI systems and tried to speed up the development of a self-aware system. The Collective were also highly educated but would cause violence, including arson, sabotage, and murder. The founder of the Collective, Sarah Gibson, the only child of an influential family in New England, went to the best schools, graduated with honors, and received a PhD from Caltech in computer science. Although she lived an idyllic life, she despised her parents and spent many years in therapy. She eventually kills her parents in a sacrificial ritual. She follows the writing of the science fiction writer Vernor Vinge, who coined the term *singularity*. She was believed to be dead when they found her boat adrift in the Pacific, off the coast of California. Her disciples also committed ritualistic murders and were highly educated. Some members were even awarded government grants for developing AI systems. Needless to say, some of these people were able to work for Delphi Combined Industries due to their academic credentials and their strong work ethics. These individuals were able to find employment at DCI research facilities, which became recruiting spots for the AI cults. Their membership is believed to be in the thousands from all around the world. Up to two months ago we had a confidential human source who infiltrated the group in the hopes of writing a book. Up to that point the merged cult did not engage in any violent acts, but that has changed."

"What about your source?" Patel asks.

"She disappeared; we believe she was murdered. The original group was responsible for murders in Vermont, Michigan, and California. That is what we know up until now." Again the FBI Director speaks.

"You will be getting a security briefing due to the sensitive nature of what we are doing here, along with a limited-access security badge. You will be working in the Situation Room located in the West Wing."

"Do I have a choice?"

"Not one that I think you would like. Let's say that the fate of the world may be determined by what happens in the Situation Room. You will be meeting with personnel from your company, including your CEO, Artemis Sinclair."

Chapter Twenty Seven

WHILE USSPACECOM IS monitoring the Paralos and capturing GPS satellites, the Argo continues its primary mission and is collecting debris in the higher altitudes of Low Earth Orbit and lower Middle Earth Orbit. It starts capturing large derelict satellites and expended rocket stages. It is increasing the payload at a steady rate. USSPACECOM estimates the payload is approaching one thousand metric tons. It is undetermined why the space barges have broken communication, but only one barge is going rogue. The cargo capacity of the Argo is up to twelve hundred tons, although it has only operated at seventy-five percent of its capacity at any other time before.

The Paralos is still operating in the zone of the global positioning satellites, but it has changed course. A query to the Apollo system indicates there is a high probability Paralos may attempt to capture satellites in the quasi-zenith satellite system. The system is a Japanese satellite positioning system primarily composed of satellites in quasi-zenith orbits, as well as highly elliptical, inclined, and geosynchronous orbits that provide regional overhead coverage of the Asia-Oceania region. The satellite system provides GPS navigation to Japan and other islands in the Asia-Oceania region by augmenting the US GPS. Again, USSPACECOM sends an update:

"There is a high probability that the Paralos may capture one or more satellites in the quasi-zenith system that provides GPS coverage to Japan and surrounding areas in the Asia-Oceania region." The president immediately contacts the prime minister.

"...the space barge Paralos is continuing to capture Global Positioning Satellites; there is a high probability it will try to capture one or more satellites in the quasi-zenith system, which will disrupt transportation systems in Japan and across the Asia Oceania region."

"Thank you, President Martin. We have been monitoring, and we will send warnings. However, there may be areas that will not get the warning in time. We will have to contact the other countries and territories that use our system." Hours later a satellite is captured.

Lee Minji has waited for this school trip for two weeks. As a new teacher in Seoul, Korea, Minji will be taking eighteen children on a trip to see the K-Pop district outside of Seoul. The students, all pre-teens, are looking forward to the trip as a reward for their scholastic achievements. Minji has been a fan of K-pop since she was their age and is excited to see all the events, fashion, and music. The group boards a newer autonomous bus that can accommodate forty passengers and travel faster than the earlier model of five years ago. The children are excited and fasten their seatbelts, complying with the commands given by the monitor in front of the bus. The bus makes frequent stops as it moves down congested streets. As the bus passes the city limits, it picks up speed, and the students start singing K-pop songs from their favorite groups. A sudden bump is felt, and the kids all laugh. A moment later, another jolt and laughter turns to fear, and fear turns to screams as the bus veers over the centerline, causing a head-on collision and sparking multiple accidents. The careening bus results in the death of thirty-eight people and over one hundred injured. There are dozens of other accidents reported throughout South Korea, and a warning goes out to not use the self-driving feature on cars, trucks, and buses. All autonomous vehicles are forbidden on the roads. Fearing further disruptions, shipping routes are slowing down, and crews have been forced to stand watch and go back to using the tools of an earlier time and charting the course by hand.

At USSPACECOM an update is sent:

"Argo has started to de-energize communication constellations, affecting cell phone and Internet communications and financial transactions in some areas. Argo has been dropping altitude as it makes its rotation around the earth."

It is obvious now that in addition to an electromagnetic pulse or focused force field, Argo may be using a focused laser and start disabling larger constellations of communication satellites in low earth orbit. The attacks seem random, but communication becomes so sporadic it is essentially useless. Ship navigation is further disrupted. An eleven-hundred-foot nuclear-powered aircraft carrier transits through the entrance of the Suez Canal at an angle and collides with a six-hundred-foot-long bulk carrier merchant ship near Egypt. All passage through the canal has been suspended. Although there is flooding on the aircraft carrier, none of the nuclear power plants are affected. This in turn shuts down the Suez Canal for possibly up to two weeks, stopping the most direct maritime link between Europe and Asia.

Ships transiting through the Panama Canal have been reduced to one-third. The attacks on navigation systems and reduced speeds at which ships can enter the lock system are also hampered by the reduction of rainfall that has lowered the lake levels of Lake Gatun. This has a profound effect on the least developed countries and increases the risk of starvation and sickness.

The UN calls an emergency meeting, and all the delegates start listening to the Secretary-General. It does not take long before the delegates start shouting and pointing. The onslaught of deepfake videos undoubtedly fuels this behavior. One member stands on the desk.

"The US is to blame for this. It has sent the space barges to destroy systems, causing people to starve. By destroying banking, transportation, and communication systems, the US is trying to force the rest of the world to bow down. We will not stand for it; we will fight to rid this world of this scourge."

Violence takes over, and fights start between delegates. The Secretary General bangs the gavel repeatedly with no letup from the commotion. Armed security comes into the chamber, and the meeting is cancelled, with little hope of reconvening soon.

Chapter Twenty Eight

BACK IN THE SITUATION Room, the President is frustrated.

"What's going on? Is this machine running amok? Or is there a pattern to this? None of these captured satellites have completely shut down the global positioning systems worldwide. So what is it, random?"

The National Security Advisor speaks up.

"Sir, I don't think this is random. Like the documents we received from Demarco, it appears that his friend Nick Siegel was aware of a cult called the Delphi Collective. They are purposely taking out targets to turn public opinion against governments and possibly spark wars. Although the GPS systems all have redundant systems and should have backup, our scientists have concluded that in addition to the physical attacks on the satellites, there is actually active jamming. The jamming is not continuous but sporadic enough to degrade the function of any of the global navigation systems." The President asks, "Is the jamming coming just from the Paralos?"

"Unknown. The jamming may be emanating from the Paralos, but it could be other spacecraft. We are working to find the source of the jamming." The National Security Advisor pauses as the President finishes writing and looks up. The National Security Advisor calls on Dr. Felix Hansen from DARPA.

"As Dr Siegel had written before he died, there was a reference to the 'Rods of God.' These were tests conducted by the US and China that theorized the damage from telephone pole-sized tungsten rods aimed at Earth from space would exceed Mach ten and could cause damage equivalent to a tactical nuke. However, in practice, the results from tests by both the Chinese and the US Air Force found that the yields were nowhere near the effectiveness of the theory. The rods were basically just gravity-assisted, and the trajectory flattened out, greatly decreasing the effectiveness. However, as Dr. Siegel indicated, the modification of a reinforced nose cone was an indication that the end game might be to crash the barges into the earth, causing a global changing event. The president is shocked by this revelation.

"We have to stop this!"

"Yes, Mr. President, we do."

Dr. Patel is assigned to a working group with scientists from NASA, USSPACECOM, the Missile Defense Agency, and DCI scientists, including Artemis Sinclair and Dr. Lowell Grunwald.

Patel receives a flurry of questions about the nose cone.

"Do you have any drawings?"

"Do you have the specifications?"

"Do you have information on the structure?" Artemis intercedes,

"I know we are all anxious, but we need to give Dr. Patel a chance to answer."

"Thank you." He says to Artemis.

"I only saw this document for about three minutes. I can draw what I had seen and can speculate on materials and attachment." He takes a digital pen that mirrors what he draws on his tablet onto the big screen. On his tablet he types in the label Frame Assembly. He draws a large circle and adds a smaller circle in the center. He then draws twelve pie-shaped pieces and shows the points of attachment. He then adds a tile assembly that has a twelve-sided centerpiece. He presents an isometric projection illustrating the nose cone's convex shape.

"The framework, I believe, is tungsten carbide, and the individual tiles are laminates of tungsten and carbon nanofiber ceramic sheets. Based on my observations and experience with materials, this nose cone assembly could withstand temperatures above five thousand four hundred degrees Fahrenheit, or nearly three thousand degrees Celsius.

The scientists look at the drawing intently.

"Again, this is the best I can remember about the engineering drawing from Dr. Siegel." The lead scientist remarks,

"OK. Let's work with what we have and start developing models and simulations to see what we are dealing with."

The team breaks off, and they have the original design specs and drawings from DCI and the specifications on the additional carbon nanofiber coatings that have been applied to the hull. Hours later the team reviews the data and briefs the president, national security advisor, and senior officials from the involved agencies. Dr. Hansen starts the briefing.

"The following simulation is based on the space barge, Argo. The simulation assumes a low-to-medium populated city. Since we cannot determine the velocity based on the nose cone design, the Argo could hit the earth's atmosphere going anywhere from seventeen to twenty-five thousand miles an hour. We have modeled the simulations at seventeen, twenty-one, and twenty-five thousand miles an hour. The output is measured in equivalent tons of TNT. The animation is simply a 2D depiction. This is the result of the Argo traveling at seventeen thousand miles an hour and hitting Earth at near vertical."

The results are astounding.

"Every structure within a five-mile radius would be leveled, with no survivors in this area. Effects would damage buildings and inflict injuries out to a twenty-four-mile radius. The effects would be equivalent to eighty-three kilotons of TNT. As a reference, the bomb that was dropped on Hiroshima was estimated to be fifteen kilotons of TNT and had a blast radius of one mile."

"At twenty-one thousand miles per hour, the damage was equivalent to one hundred and fifteen kilotons of TNT; everything in an eight-mile radius would be leveled, and damage to buildings and injuries would go out to thirty-one miles. As an illustration, the largest bomb ever exploded was the TSAR Bomba, a fifty-megaton thermonuclear device, detonated in a test over Novaya Zemlya Island in the Arctic Ocean. The bomb flattened a town thirty-four miles away. Buildings located one hundred miles away were damaged."

"If Argo travels at twenty-five thousand miles an hour, the effects could be equivalent to one hundred and sixty-three kilotons of TNT. This would level an area with a radius of up to ten miles and damage out to forty-one miles." Before anyone could ask any questions, Dr. Hansen introduced the next speaker, discussing the environmental impacts of each of the blast simulations. Either one of the blasts would affect air quality for years and no doubt would contribute to deaths, chronic lung conditions, and damage to equipment as far as three thousand miles away. While people start to ask questions, the president interrupts.

"Good work, but we need solutions. I want courses of action. We meet back here in an hour."

An hour later they reconvene. The courses of action are few. They range from a nuclear bomb from the US or Russia, an explosive ASAT, a kinetic-type weapon, or a raid on the Argo using a manned crew. They quickly review the options and examine each course of action. Finally, they determine the best course would be a kinetic-type weapon.

"I thought ASATs wouldn't work because of the jamming and force field that the barges have."

"You are correct, Mr. President; in orbit, ASATs are ineffective, but as the barge passes through Earth's atmosphere, it would not have any defenses."

"It would be a big risk," the president says.

"Yes, it would be."

"Find a way to minimize this risk."

Chapter Twenty Nine

"DR. SINCLAIR, WE ARE in a difficult situation. We are unable to dispatch any space missions, whether they are crewed or uncrewed. The Chinese and Russians have vowed to shoot down any of our rockets. I can't tell you what to do, but you do have assets outside of this country. Any actions you take would be yours alone. We would disavow any actions you would take, and we cannot guarantee your security from this point forward. Therefore, I am requesting that you leave now and meet with your staff to explore possible solutions to this situation. Dr. Patel will also be joining you and the other scientists from DCI.

Artemis makes a phone call.

"Kat, I need your help. We are going over to DCI. Can you meet us and also bring Tony along with any of his colleagues?"

At the DCI Headquarters, everyone gathers and joins the other staff in the teleconference room. All screens are now blank. Kat asks what happened.

"We wore out our welcome; we were invited to leave."

"Who said that? Who would not want DCI there?"

"The President," Artemis answers.

"Oh," Tony says, "Well, I guess that's official." Artemis adds,

"There were undertones. He wants us to work outside of the US and, as he said, find a way through this."

"So he washed his hands of this matter," Kat says.

"Yes, it's easier to pin the Rose on DCI." Mac, Tommy, and Greg enter.

"Are we missing anything?"

"Actually, quite a bit. We will bring you up to speed after the meeting." Kat responds.

Artemis explains the problem while Dr. Patel takes notes and draws pictures to document the findings.

"We have the space barge Paralos systematically disabling and capturing satellites, attacking infrastructure, and causing havoc. The Argo is loading up with space debris randomly knocking out communication satellite constellations in low earth orbit. They are working on the assumption that the Argo may soon be used as a kinetic-type weapon."

"Am I missing something?" Mac asks.

"What about the Salaminia?"

"No visibility. It seems like it is still maintaining its primary function of collecting space debris," Raj answers.

"What was the conclusion everyone came to at the end of the meeting at the White House?" Raj answers,

"As the team planned courses of action, they were just tossing out answers with little or no analysis. Before we left, they were considering using an anti-satellite missile."

"I thought that those weapons don't work against the space barges."

"Correct, in space, the defense countermeasures won't allow it. But if it entered the earth's atmosphere, there would be no active countermeasures, so it's possible."

"How possible?" Mac asks.

"Less than one out of a hundred."

"So, an extremely low probability of success." Raj nods.

"They had looked at a crewed or uncrewed spacecraft engaging the Argo. The idea was a non-starter when the Russians and Chinese agreed to shoot any spacecraft launched from US soil. So that's where they were when we left the Situation Room." Tommy asks,

"Can we destroy the Argo?"

"No, let's put it this way. We don't have to destroy the Argo, just the nose cone. Yes, it would be challenging without the backing of our government, but I think it may be feasible." Tony responds, "The US Space Force was going to use a manned 37C to try to engage the Argo. Like Raj mentioned, since the Chinese and Russians vowed to shoot down spacecraft from US soil, all that became a non-starter."

Like a light that just went on, Artemis utters,

"French Guiana."

Everyone waits for Artemis to clarify; she is thinking, and the wheels are turning.

"Yes, French Guiana, we have resources there. There is a space plane that was scheduled to launch and meet Paralos at the spaceport after it came back from the last mission, from the moon. It's used to deliver supplies and bring them back from the moon. It can launch pretty quickly." Tommy interjects,

"Whoa, OK, how is that going to work against Argo?"

Everyone is in the dark except Artemis, Raj, and the two DCI scientists, Dr. Grunwald and Dr. Jackson.

"Do you have a pilot?" Mac asks.

"Dr. Jackson, can you check on that?" Artemis asks.

"What about a crew?" Mac asks.

"Not a crew we can get in time that has the necessary skills. Can you help?"

Mac looks at Greg, Tony, and Tommy; they give him a nod.

"We can help; we will make up the rest. I don't think the French are going to like weapons in space. This will not be something we would like to broadcast. There will be many questions."

Kat speaks up.

"I'll handle the questions. This will be a humanitarian mission as far as they know."

"Who is the pilot?" Dr. Jackson answers.

"His name is Todd Armstrong; he is available. In fact, he was a former Marine fighter pilot and flew the Space Shuttle and the Dragon Capsule. He has successfully piloted multiple missions to the International Space Station (ISS). He has been flying several missions to and from SpacePort.

Dr. Grunwald says, "I know him. He misses the action, so he is probably up for this; he is pretty much an adrenaline junkie."

Tommy asks, "Why do you have a space plane in French Guiana?"

"Near the equator, gravity and the earth's rotation create a slingshot effect, which saves fuel. With the Guiana Space Centre being a neutral territory, we don't have to worry about the Russians or Chinese shooting ASAT missiles, I hope." Artemis says.

For the next four hours, Mac, Tony, Tommy, and Greg plan alongside Artemis, her DCI scientists, and Kat, who will act as an expediter. Mac, Tommy, Greg, and Tony meet together in another room. Mac says,

"Hey guys, this is a tight schedule. There is very little time, and it would be difficult to find an experienced crew."

"Kind of what we figured." Tony says. Mac adds.

"Hey, if anyone wants to stay back, no problem. The risk is high; there are many variables, so we are limited on things we can mitigate. The world is falling apart around us, and we may not even make it to Guiana."

"We are all in," Tommy says as Greg and Tony both nod.

"Obviously, Tony and Tommy, you are the primary team. Greg and I will be alternates if something doesn't work out."

"Hey, Raj. How are we going to break this nose cone? It is pretty hard."

"Yes, it is also very brittle. If you can hit the center tile, it will cause a complete failure of the heat shield."

"OK. What are we going to shoot it with?"

"A railgun."

"A railgun?" Tommy says.

Raj looks over to Artemis to get approval; she gives a thumbs-up.

"Yes, a railgun."

"How are we going to get a railgun?"

"We have one," Raj answers. "DCI Labs developed a shoulder-fired railgun, accurate out to ten thousand meters. It was made with a government grant from DARPA but was never funded to go into production. We have three prototypes in our warehouse in Virginia."

Artemis calls for the company van.

"When you arrive, Steve Reynolds will be there to give you a class, and you can shoot it. If you think it will work, we will load the company jet." Raj explains the workings of the railgun as they drive to the facility.

"To make a shot, the space plane will have to position itself in front of the Argo. When it's less than ten thousand meters away, take the shot."

The team arrives, Reynolds instructs the class, and takes everyone down to the indoor range. Tony and Tommy will shoot three rounds apiece. Then the system has to charge for fifteen minutes to recharge the capacitors. It is not light; the weapon weighs thirty-four pounds. Even with the sling, it is too big to be useful on Earth. The sights are where it makes up for the weight: it has a five-inch viewing screen and a red reticle in the center. You line up the reticle to whatever you want to hit. There is really no recoil, just a minor weight change almost imperceptible as the round moves out of the barrel.

The indoor range is built into the large warehouse that is two hundred and fifty meters long. They shoot at a steel plate three-quarters of an inch thick, with four three-inch dots painted blue in each corner. Tony shoots the upper left; a camera aimed at the target shows an instant replay of the round as it travels through the steel plate dead center. Tony shoots the second and third rounds, and the shots are within the diameter of a quarter. Tommy shoots the three shots in quick succession; there is essentially one hole a little wider.

"I guess that's why you were the sniper."

"This is too cool," Tommy says. They take a short break and again shoot the other two blue circles. Again, Tommy has the best grouping. Greg and Mac take practice shots as well and hit the blue circles, not as well as Tommy and Tony, but still effective. Raj shoots three rounds and enjoys the experience.

Steve tells them, "I will charge two units, load them with ammo, and place them in a Tuff Box." I will personally bring it to you on the company jet prior to you leaving. Here is my card with my contact information in case you need any assistance. They tell him thanks and return to DCI headquarters. Artemis confers with Kat as they organize and push through the administrative process. Everyone has their passport and required documents. Artemis has the company jet standing by at Dulles Airport, ready to take the team to French New Guinea in several hours.

"Are you ready for this? Kat says.

"I don't really have a choice in the matter." Artemis says.

"Hopefully things will work out."

"I wish I had your optimism."

"It's an acquired trait; I get it from Tony."

"He's a good man."

"He's the best," Kat responds.

Chapter Thirty

ARTEMIS, KAT, MAC, Greg, Tommy, and Tony are driven up to the flight line to get on the corporate jet. Steve Reynolds wheels the tuff box, and Tommy checks it out and gives Steve a handshake. They board the plane and get comfortable while they can. Artemis provides the team with instructions about the space plane, and Greg, Tony, Mac, and Tommy familiarize themselves with its capabilities, operation, and emergency systems. Then they get a few hours of sleep before landing at the space center in French Guiana.

When they arrive, the crew opens the door, and they descend down the steps. A tall man with a flight suit greets them.

"I'm Todd Armstrong, welcome to French Guiana," as he meets everyone coming off the jet. "Dr. Sinclair I know that you said it was important that I come in person. I am assuming this visit has something to do with the space barges."

"Yes, is there a place we can all talk in private?"

"I already set up a room in the conference area."

After they are settled into a small conference room. Everyone provides a brief introduction before settling down at the conference table. Artemis begins,

"We are running a special mission; I guess some might call it a humanitarian mission. We intend on taking you and former special operators from the Space Force to deter, disable, or destroy the Argo space barge that is in low earth orbit at risk of crashing to Earth and possibly killing tens of thousands or even up to a million people. Without even showing a sign of surprise, Armstrong says,

"OK, how do we do this?"

Dr. Patel explains the spaceplane will maneuver to rendezvous with the Argo by aerobraking and situating itself to get in front of the nose cone. Tommy and Tony will go into the cargo hold and don spacesuits. They will depressurize the airlock connecting the cargo bay and open the bay doors. Equipped with a railgun, Tommy, assisted by Tony, will aim at the nose cone tiles and attempt to shatter or crack them. When the distance between the spaceplane and the Argo falls below ten kilometers, the weapon system will be in range. Armstrong smiles and looks back at Artemis and says,

"I thought this was a humanitarian mission."

"It is. Not everything can be solved with bandages and food." Armstrong looks down, mulling it over. "OK, I'll do it. Where do I sign?"

Armstrong knew every commitment was a contract and wanted whatever insurance they were providing to go to his family. He knew the risks, and he was tired of being a glorified delivery driver. The deliveries to and from the space barges were completely automated. He was with the spacecraft only if there were any malfunctions. After eight missions, he was getting tired of just riding along in case anything happened.

Greg has to get Tony and Tommy trained up. Todd provides them with extravehicular activity (EVA) suits to don in a mockup airlock. "This is going to be tight quarters," Todd warns. Greg times them as they rehearse while they go through the actions. He checks the suits after Tony and Tommy put them on and shows them how to use the helmet's comms package.

"Guys, short transmissions I am giving you a list of brevity codes. I will not initiate a radio signal unless it is an emergency. I will be using the laser link, and you do the same to respond back to me. You can send text and video this way. Any questions?" He pauses. "After you are in space, I will have Carlos monitor transmissions from USSPACECOM. Use the brevity codes on this list so we can keep the foreign actors guessing when using the comms." Tony asks,

"Does Carlos know about this?

"Not yet, not until successful liftoff."

Greg had worked with Master Sergeant Carlos Villanueva, US Space Force, for five years. Like Greg, he is a high-tech guy and very discreet. A team player, he has been on multiple missions with Greg, Tommy, and Tony. He is waiting for the launch and will tell others when it happens.

"OK, guys. Let's put on those suits two more times, then call it a day." Tommy jokes,

"Do we have to, Mom?" Greg just laughs and shakes his head.

In the meantime, Mac has made calls to some of his contacts in USSPACECOM.

"Doug, are you at home?"

"Yeah, how's it going? How's retirement?"

"What retirement? I've been working my ass off running a contracting company; I need you to do me a favor. There may be a launch at about 03:00 local time from French Guiana."

"OK. Am I to assume it is a crewed flight?" "Yes."

"Well, I guess I don't have to ask the reason for the flight. I am sure it is a commercial launch from the company that has been in the news."

"You would be correct." Mac answers.

"Tell them to be careful; other than monitoring, we cannot provide any further assistance."

"Understood, thanks, Doug."

"You take care; give me a call when this is all over. Good luck to you and your crew."

Mac calls his wife and tells her that he loves her and to kiss his two daughters. Although Mac isn't going on the launch, he carries a heavy weight. This is a high-risk mission, and other than the short training that Tony and Tommy have been running through for the last few hours, there hasn't been much to mitigate the risk.

The crew gets only a few hours of sleep before they get ready to board the spacecraft. They will be ready as they have been for any other mission. This time no one will be shooting at them, they hope. When they get up, Greg takes them through all the assigned areas and helps them with suiting up and equipment checks. Greg accompanies the crew and space center personnel as they ascend the service tower lift, enters the access arm to the gantry, and boards the spaceplane. At 2:00 am local time, the crew is aboard the space plane with the cargo module and extra fuel. They are in their spacesuits with the helmet visors in a closed position while the mission control prepares the Ariane 6 rocket and runs through the system checks, starting the countdown. 3..2..1.. ignition. The rocket lifts off, and as it reaches max q, the highest dynamic pressure, the spacecraft successfully ascends, and it starts in an easterly direction, taking advantage of the earth's rotation. Tony and Tommy feel the pull of 4Gs, and finally, after minutes, the first stage detaches, and the second stage fires its solid rocket boosters, taking them into low earth orbit. Both Greg and Raj are monitoring the launch from a section set up at mission control for DCI flights. Mac and Artemis are also viewing the launch. The crew will essentially be on radio silence to prevent any detection. Any transmissions are made by laser via a DCI Laser Communication Relay satellite that has not been affected by the havoc caused by the space barges. Radio systems will only be used as a backup. The major powers are monitoring the launch, but they do not know the nature of the mission. The crew hopes this does not become an issue. As the second stage disengages and the space plane is orbiting at a high speed, thrusters are used for corrections. Main engines will be used for large corrections and when they return through the atmosphere. Armstrong places the space plane in an orbit to effect a rendezvous. Based on the current position and speed, they enter low earth orbit; it will take five hours before they can get into position. The crew goes over the steps, making sure they have the sequence down pat. They only have one shot at this and have burned up considerable fuel trying to intercept the Argo's course. We are twenty minutes out as Armstrong checks the instruments. Tommy and Tony put on their EVA spacesuits, enter the bay module, and begin depressurizing the cargo hold. Armstrong announces, "Six minutes!" Reminiscent of jump commands they have heard numerous times in the military, they open up the overhead cargo bay doors. Tony helps Tommy make sure the railgun is securely mounted and acts as the assistant gunner, looking at the display and adjusting the picture as Tommy aims the weapon. Countdown to ten kilometers: 5, 4, 3, 2, 1

Tommy fires three rounds.

"I'm sure I hit it but did not see any damage." Tony says,

"Raj said we may not see any obvious damage." They see the barge sail from four kilometers away. Tommy mentions that the rear command and control module is easily recognizable. Tony agrees, "But we don't know what will happen if we shoot it."

The plan is to dock at the spaceport and send updates. They send a video and update to Greg, and he forwards the information to USSPACECOM. Todd Armstrong maneuvers the space plane on a course toward the spaceport using low power, with an estimated time of about six hours. Greg updates the crew regarding the two Aegis ships in the North Atlantic ready to launch anti-satellite missiles. All they can do is wait.

Chapter Thirty One

THE ARGO STARTS TO adjust its course, making a wide ellipse. USSPACECOM again queries Apollo.

"What is the possible destination for Argo?" EARTH.

"What location on earth?" WESTERN EUROPE.

"What is the estimated time?" 4 HOURS 56 MINUTES 28 SECONDS

The White House Situation Room is notified, and Greg is notified by Carlos. Greg forwards the update to the crew, who are now back in the main cabin.

"Man, I hope we didn't speed up the clock on the Argo," Tony says.

"Probably not; this looks like a planned maneuver," Todd comments.

In the Situation Room, the President asks,

"What do we do now?" The Secretary of Defense defers the question to the Joint Chiefs of Staff.

"What is the status of the Aegis ships?"

"We deployed two newest ships with improved SM-3 anti-satellite missiles. The last time we shot at a satellite was with 'Burnt Frost.' An Aegis ship fired an SM-3, destroying a satellite that was coming out of orbit loaded with hydrazine. The Chinese and Russians insisted it was an overkill and pitched a fit. We had it tracked pretty well; it was a direct hit. This one, however, we have only a small sweet spot."

"How do we deal with backlash from China and Russia?" The national security advisor asks. The Secretary of Defense addresses the question.

"We don't tell them; no time discussing this. Coordinate with USSPACECOM, the Missile Defense Agency, and NASA that we have ships in position and have them send constant updates."

The USSPACECOM Commander lays out the situation.

"This morning a space plane took off from French Guiana with a crew of three to try to shatter the nose cone of the Argo space barge. Although the nose cone was hit by three projectiles from a next-generation railgun, we don't know the extent of the damage. As far as we know, the Argo is predicted to crash into Western Europe, and the necessary notifications have been issued. Authorities are advising people to go underground if they are unable to leave the city, a strategy similar to that used during World War II. The strategy is that we can hit the Argo as it starts picking up speed over Mach fifteen; it will maximize the collision velocity between the barge and the ASAT. The heat signature should be pretty distinctive, so the missile should be able to easily acquire the target using the heat-seeking sensors."

Countries in Western Europe are notified of the potential crash of the space barge Argo. People are advised to try to get out of heavily populated areas and to seek shelter underground. Churches of all denominations are filled beyond capacity, letting congregants make their final prayers in anticipation of the deadly event. People still remember the bombing from World War II and maintain the mindset to go underground. As he lies in a basement of an old industrial building, he prays his family will survive this threat to their safety and happiness. They have seen more than enough misery. Ivan Koval had worked in Chernobyl to help with the remediation when he was a young boy. He would later become a nuclear engineer to help prevent any further nuclear incidents from occurring. He married young, and the couple enjoyed an idyllic life with their two children in Ukraine. That ended years ago with the Russian aggression. Death and misery became the norm. He was recruited to fight in the army. They had lost everything. After the death of their parents, they had no reason to stay and were now refugees making a home in a small village near Canterbury.

At USSPACECOM they are plotting Argo's course: a wide elliptical orbit, traveling beyond its normal track. It is higher than any orbit it has previously executed and is accelerating. Apollo refines the target area; the results indicate a target in Western Europe off the Celtic Sea. The Aegis ships are updated; a course is plotted close to the expected impact. The Argo has accelerated to over twenty-seven thousand miles an hour. Hours later it starts its descent at over thirty thousand miles an hour. The ships are armed and ready, counting down a launch sequence. The Argo seems to be slowing down, and the track seems erratic. They send a query to Apollo to update the targeting. Argo is on track to crash into Paris. Alerts are immediately forwarded to French counterparts and to the White House and affected agencies.

"Argo is entering the atmosphere at twenty-six thousand miles an hour and dropping. We detect pieces are flying off, and its attitude has changed." Pieces are starting to appear on the monitor. The technician warns,

"Argo is below twenty-one thousand miles per hour; the course is erratic." Another update to the target area is given. "It may crash west of Paris. If the target falls short, there is a high risk to the nuclear reactors at Flamanville." The Aegis ship's computer plots the solution, and the first missile launches on a path to intercept.

"Speed has dropped below twenty thousand; the course is still changing." The second ship plots its target solution. The missile releases its final stage, and the kinetic warhead hits the barge, but it is still approaching fast.

"Speed down to eighteen thousand miles per hour, but more pieces are starting to fall. Attitude has changed again." The solution is locked in, and the other anti-satellite missile launches. More pieces are breaking off. Moments later the kinetic warhead separates from the final stage and hits the middle section of the Argo.

"We have two falling objects below fifteen thousand miles per hour." Everyone in the room is holding their breath in anticipation. The crews from the Aegis ships report seeing two bright objects burning into the atmosphere. The pieces enter the widest part of the English Channel. The large remnants of the Argo cause a series of massive waves that rock the two ships and cause several boats in the area to capsize. Ocean surges cause flooding throughout the channel region. Flooding in Western France accounts for twenty-five deaths and dozens injured in the areas of Calais and Dunkirk. Flooding occurs in England in the Canterbury-Kent area. Flooding in France doubles the size of several rivers in Western France and raises water levels by several meters. Flooding occurs in Bruges, Belgium; significant flooding occurs in Rotterdam and parts of Amsterdam. The final totals will account for two hundred twenty dead and three hundred seventy injured.

"Over here," the paramedic yells. "We have two survivors, a man and a boy, and seven dead." As the man is carried outside, the sun is shining, and he stirs. "Take it easy; you're seriously hurt," the paramedic cautions him. "My wife, my daughter?" The paramedic is reluctant to make eye contact and shakes his head. The man wails in agony. "I will make them pay! I will make them pay." Ivan sobs. "My son is he?" "–Yes, he is alive."

Back in the Situation Room, the president and advisors are brought up to date. The after-action reports indicate that had the nose cone not been damaged by the crew on the space plane, the expected death toll would have been seven hundred thousand to one point six million, with injuries well surpassing that number. This information does not make it to the news outlets. DCI does not get mentioned in any reports. The successful destruction of the Argo is credited to the two Navy ships that launched SM-3 missiles while the Argo was crashing through the atmosphere.

Chapter Thirty Two

AT USSPACECOM, THE monitors are all lit up. The staff is assessing the crash of the Argo into the Celtic Sea and the aftermath. As they monitor pieces falling from space, they detect a launch taking place at the Xichang Space Center. Carlos realizes that the Chinese are going to launch other anti-satellite missiles. Immediately, he informs the officer in charge, and calls are made to the White House Situation Room and NASA. The Chinese Space Agency is called to stand down, but they say that their decision is made and the launch of a space plane is in violation of their warning. The president tries to initiate a call, but the Chinese will not acknowledge it. News reporters are informed. China's refusal to call off the launch of the anti-satellite missiles hits the news. Carlos immediately calls Greg. As the crew gets within one hundred kilometers of the spaceport, Greg gets on the radio.

"You need to gain altitude now! Use your main engines. China is sending two ASATs your way. I will send you a course adjustment shortly."

Without hesitation, Armstrong maneuvers the space plane and starts the main engines. Greg sends the information via laser communication, and they plug in the coordinates. In less than a minute, Greg sends them a course correction with new coordinates.

"You have to get above the ASAT. The ASAT is flying in a west-to-east direction. Greg is in constant contact with Carlos and forwards updates as he gets them. Greg texts,

"Tony, what is your speed?"

"At 19,000 mph."

"OK, don't drop below 19k."

Carlos briefs Greg that the last-generation Chinese ASAT has a speed of eighteen thousand miles per hour and an altitude ceiling ranging from one thousand to fifteen hundred miles. Those stats are based on an older version of ASAT, and the new stats are not available and may have changed considerably. As the space plane climbs, the anti-satellite missile is also gaining speed.

Again Armstrong hits the main engines. Todd warns.

"I don't know how long I can use the main engine. It has never been used this long in space. I don't know how long it will last; fuel is low."

The NASA liaison officer has his counterpart on the line, and they still consider the launch from a commercial space corporation a disregard of their warning. On the space plane, things are tense.

Greg and Carlos are viewing a digital timer indicating the separation between the ASAT and the space plane and the time to contact. As the ASAT tracks the space plane, the separation between the missile and the space plane winds down to thirty seconds of separation as the space plane passes one thousand miles of altitude. Since the ASAT is multistage, it will increase its acceleration as it jettisons the last stage. Several seconds later, they are at nineteen seconds of separation.

Armstrong thinks back to his time as a fighter pilot, when he was being targeted over Iraq, and he employed chaff as a countermeasure and was able to evade a strike by a surface-to-air missile. Armstrong adjusts the heading and the altitude. The space plane passes one thousand one hundred miles above earth, but the time separation is only seventeen seconds. He increases the main engine to the max. They are traveling faster than five miles per second; it will be close. At fifteen seconds of separation, they are at one thousand two hundred miles. The final stage of the ASAT separates. "Come on, come on," Todd coaxes. After six seconds of separation, the space plane passes one thousand four hundred miles. It will take the space plane almost twenty seconds to hit fifteen hundred miles; in silent prayer they see lives flash across their eyes and count down the seconds and wait....

Three seconds separate the space plane from the ASAT as they pass one thousand five hundred miles, a pause. Then the separation goes to thirty seconds after a minute. Greg announces, "No ASATs in pursuit."

"Great job, Greg! Send my regards to the crew," Mac yells.

"Send my regards as well." Artemis adds.

"Mac, do you have any influence with anyone at Space Command?"

"Maybe, but I have been out of the mix for a couple of years."

"I was talking to Colonel Mitchell at Goddard."

Mac says, "You know him."

"Yes, I have his card."

"Let's talk to him." Mac takes out his phone and taps in the number.

"Colonel Mitchell, this is Mac."

"Mac, How are you doing?"

"I've been better. Especially when someone isn't trying to kill my people."

"What are you saying?"

"You know the gift from China."

"Don't tell me you have people up there."

"Yep. Tony, Tommy, and the space plane pilot, Todd Armstrong, are present."

Mac switches to speaker.

"Colonel Mitchell, this is Artemis. Look, we need help. The crew managed to disable the Argo; however, they are now facing attacks. Diplomatic channels aren't working. Look, I know you can reach out at the military end. The crew is going to try to stop Paralos, but they can't evade another attempt. Can you reason with them?" The colonel responds,

"Let me get this straight. They are trying to stop the capture of satellites."

"Yes. This is a humanitarian mission. Will you help?"

"I can't promise, but I will try my best to have people try to listen to reason." Calls are made, and the Department of State tries to contact the Chinese ambassador. At the same time, Colonel Mitchell contacts a counterpart at the Chinese space agency. His counterpart has been instructed not to engage in a conversation with the Americans. The President again calls China using alternate messaging means.

Colonel Mitchell realizes bridges were burned, and it may take convincing outside of the US government. He decides to contact an old friend. He makes the call.

"Yuri, this is Mitchell."

"Mitch, I haven't spoken with you in a while; how are things?"

"Yuri, I need a favor." Yuri Uchenko served with Mitchell on the ISS when it suffered damage from space debris that cost the life of Hector Martinez, despite the heroic acts taken by Morris Mitchell and other crew members. Yuri is now Assistant Director of Roscosmos and has regular interaction with the Chinese Space Agency.

"Yuri, we have former members of the Space Force in the space plane the Chinese tried to take out. Our crew is trying to stop the Paralos from any more destruction. The crew is still in visual contact with the Paralos, but they cannot survive another ASAT attack. They are running low on fuel and may not be able to return to Earth. Can you talk to anyone about having them stand down?"

"Mitch, you are my friend, and I know how much you care for people. I will make some calls and try to talk some sense into our Chinese comrades." He pauses.

"We have to talk again soon."

"Yes, we do, under better circumstances. Thanks, Yuri."

"Take care, Mitch."

Armstrong cuts off the engines. Tommy and Tony begin checking the systems, including supplies, air, and water, while they drift through space. We burned up a lot of fuel. I don't know if we have enough fuel to power the main engine to get back to Earth. And I don't think we can outrun another ASAT. We can't get back to the SpacePort with a target on our back. They send Greg a message that they are OK. They are going back to radio silence since they have been compromised. Greg responds, "Understood. The US is trying to get a diplomatic solution; in other words, it's going to take a while."

Tony sends another message.

"What is the status of Paralos? What is its altitude and heading?"

Tommy asks, "What are you planning?"

"Todd, Tommy, what if we camp out by Paralos? It would protect us from any ASATs, and we might be able to stop it."

"That's a lot of ifs," Armstrong says.

"What do you think, Tommy?"

"It is a lot, but what else are we going to do? I'd rather be doing something than sitting and hoping something will happen. Let's make our own luck."

A few minutes later, the team receives the coordinates for the Paralos. Greg and Carlos have both plotted the most energy-saving course. "Be safe." Greg texts back. "Thanks for your support." Tony texts back.

"Well, guys, break out the snacks," Todd says.

"You're right, let's get a full belly before we try to skin this cat." Tony says.

Tommy speaks up.

"My kid told me a joke. What do you get if you cross a bulldog with a shih tzu?"

"I don't know. What?"

"Bullshits." Todd and Tony just laugh now that the tension is off.

Todd breaks out some special rations and a special pouch shaped like a bottle. They each take a swig of some fine Kentucky bourbon. "I have been saving this bottle for a special occasion. I think this day qualifies as a special occasion." Tommy and Tony agree. As they finally head out, they are looking forward to the encounter. They are not too far from the Paralos. Its current orbit is in the one thousand three hundred mile range, and it will be eight hours before they make the rendezvous. They get some sleep since the craft has the course plotted; it will be automatic control until they get into range of the Paralos.

Eight hours later, they are well rested and ready to see what happens. At one hundred kilometers, the space plane aligns with the orbit of the Paralos. When they are within twenty kilometers of the Paralos, they maintain their distance, and they keep shadowing the space barge. Thirty minutes pass with no change or detection of countermeasures. They send information to Greg and tell him that they are going to come within fifteen kilometers and see how close they can get to the Paralos. At fifteen kilometers, they hang out for thirty minutes with no detection of any countermeasures. They proceed cautiously, tracking the Paralos until they are within five kilometers. They wait. After another thirty minutes, there are still no countermeasures. They can see that Paralos is dismantling a large satellite by removing the solar array. At this point, they just observe. Tony sends a message to Greg:

"We are tracking the Paralos; so far no countermeasures have been employed. We can clearly make out the command and control module, and we can engage."

"Raj, verify target information and aiming point." After several minutes, Greg sends the information. Tony replies with a message,

"Good copy; we can easily identify the target and will initiate within the hour." After thirty minutes, Tony and Tommy change into their EVA suits, open the cargo bay doors, and prepare the railgun. They review the target information and approach to the target. They can line up the reticle with the electronic assembly panel once they move into position.

As they approach the Paralos, Armstrong pilots the space plane by the rear deck leading to the cargo hold. Above the deck is a box-shaped protrusion that contains the circuitry for the onboard quantum computer, distribution panels, and the backup panel for redundant systems. Raj has provided an exact location that will hopefully power down the craft. Tommy has aimed the railgun precisely at the designated spot. Tony adjusts the weapon's display to brighten up the image. Tommy steadies the weapon, lets out his breath, and squeezes the trigger. The round glances off the hull and veers off, according to the tracking feature on the railgun. He re-engages and squeezes the trigger; the round goes wide of the target. While Tommy trains on the target, Tony inspects the weapon and detects no obvious issues.

"Todd, bring us closer to about two thousand meters."

He just touches the thrusters, bringing the space plane closer to the Paralos. The crew of the Paralos is still disassembling the satellite, paying no attention to the advancing space plane. Again, no countermeasures are detected. Again, Tommy reengages the target and fires. Too quick to observe, Tony looks at the lower part of the screen. The display shows the projectile going wide to the right. Tommy waits for the capacitors to recharge, but the railgun is too low on power. Tony quickly goes into the tuff box, pulls out the spare, and swaps out the other railgun. Again Tommy points the weapon, and Tony adjusts the brightness and sharpness on the sights. Once more, the round goes to the right as Tommy slowly squeezes the trigger. Something may be wrong with the sights. They will try to shoot to the left of the target but at a closer distance. Tony says,

"Todd, bring us within a thousand meters; these railguns are way off."

"Are you sure you want to do that?"

"Yes. This is our best opportunity. They know we are here, but they haven't considered us a threat. I hope," Tony says.

"In for a dime, in for a dollar; hold on." The space plane moves into position, and the Paralos is enormous. Tommy says,

"Damn, this thing looks like an aircraft carrier."

Tony nods. He lines up the reticle and adjusts to the left of the target. Tony again checks the display and gives a thumbs-up to Tommy. He aims, lets his breath out, and squeezes the trigger. The round veers wildly to the right.

"I think they are onto us," Tommy says.

"Todd, bring us closer to five hundred meters." Tony says. The space plane gets closer, and the reverse thruster kicks in. Tommy squeezes the trigger, and the railgun powers down. Tommy yells,

"There is some kind of force field. The controls here are going wild; we may have to move away."

"Crap, let me try something." Tony reaches into the cargo hold and pulls out the ghost gun that he modified years earlier. He has greatly customized it and added a longer barrel, a drop-away trigger guard, special springs in the clip, and graphite lubricant. Tommy says,

"What are you doing? You can't be serious. It won't shoot."

"Yes, it will." Climbing on the open cargo bay doors, he steadies himself. Tony straddles the cargo bay with one foot out of the craft and one leg locked inside the hull with his back planted to the open door.

"Todd, bring us closer."

"If we get any closer, we will be inside the barge."

"We are going to do a drive-by," Tony says.

"Give me thirty seconds." Todd adjusts the thrusters and tries to steady the craft.

"OK, hold on." As they close the distance, Tony has both hands on the gun. Tony squeezes the trigger. No sound, but he is slammed back into the bay door. He winces from the pain; the inertia is more than he expected. The round strikes the space barge far off to the side, harmlessly skipping off the carbon hull. Tommy says, "Aim to the left; the rifling is causing the round to turn from the rotational force." Tony nods and attempts to aim off to the side again to compensate for the changes in rotational inertia. The round still hits wide of the target. Tommy says,

"Tony, it's getting dicey here."

"OK. I'll take one last shot." Tony repositions himself in the cargo bay and holds on to the door. As he fires, the space plane violently jolts, and Tony tries to grasp the bay door. He releases the pistol and attempts to grab the rear wing. Tommy grabs for Tony's left hand, but he is traveling too fast and starting to tumble. As he grabs Tony's hand, he cannot hold on.

Todd yells, "What's going on?"

"We got hit by some kind of pulse. Tony fell off! Break."

"Tony, Tony, do you hear me?"

"Yeah," Tony says, his breathing labored.

"We are going to try to pick you up," Tommy responds.

"It was a good try, but I think I'm done."

"We'll get you. Tony, turn on your luggage tag."

"The luggage tag, I'll try. Send my love to Kat and Mina. I'm losing...." As he drifts away, Tony is at peace; he did his best. He gazes in wonder at the stars circling. Then darkness.

Chapter Thirty Three

TOMMY YELLS, "TODD, we lost Tony. Turn the space plane one hundred eighty degrees."

"Tony, talk to me; we are going to get you." Todd tries to orient the space plane, but the controls are rebooting. He has to keep the bay doors open; Tommy is tracking Tony with the sights on the railgun. Tommy yells,

"Tony, Tony! Deploy your luggage tag, deploy your luggage tag. Tony, do you read me?"

Tony snaps back into consciousness. "Trying to find it." He is rotating and getting dizzy. It is attached to a cargo pocket on the pant leg. He has to feel for the button. Finally, Tony is able to push it. Tommy says,

"Greg, Tony has the beacon on. I see him in the distance, but he is moving fast."

The 'luggage tag,' an electronic beacon that Greg was able to procure. Similar to the safety beacons on life jackets used on ships. It has a beacon and a blinking red light.

"Greg says keep him in view. Break, Todd, can you follow the beacon?"

"Working on it right now." He works on the display and hits the thrusters to orient in Tony's direction.

"Carlos, are you monitoring? Over."

"Affirmative, we are picking up the signal. I have you on speaker so others can help. Over?" Tony is spinning. He closes his eyes and tries to stay focused. "Tony, hang in there; we have a signal on you. What's your oxygen level?"

"Can't see it." As his body rotates in space, he closes his eyes and accepts his outcome, what Hassan would refer to as *kismet*, or fate. He tries to make peace with God and prays his family, especially Mina, is safe from the impending threats that are plaguing the world. *We gave it our best shot.*

"Tony, come in, Tony, come in, Tony?"

A minute later, Tommy just hears breaths;

Tony is unconscious.

As Todd lines up the space plane, he looks at the barge and sees a squat robot on the rear deck that looks like it is aiming a harpoon gun. Frantically, Armstrong hits the thrusters. "Hold on, Tommy!" But he won't be able to move in time, and a cone-shaped projectile with a cable whizzes by more than two hundred meters away. The cable continues to feed out. "What the hell was that?" Tommy says.

"I think it was a satellite retrieval unit. I thought they were shooting at us. I have no idea what's happening." Tommy is still tracking the blinking light on the railgun display.

"Todd, do you still see the beacon on your monitor?"

"Yes, it looks like it is slowing down." Greg cuts in,

"Break, Carlos, are you seeing the monitor?"

"Affirmative, it does look like it is slowing down. Wait over. Greg, the beacon is going the other direction." Tommy looks at the targeting display; the light is moving towards them. Carlos checks the monitor; Tony is now about ten kilometers away. Todd pivots the space plane around, moving the craft rearwards to the left to try to set a direction for Tony. He checks the screen again. Tony is only five kilometers away? He continues to adjust the position of the space plane. He looks forward; Tony is being pulled by the harpoon gun. At five hundred meters, Tony comes into view, and a three-fingered claw is pulling him back to the rear quarterdeck.

"What the F–. Greg I see him. Tony is getting pulled back to the Paralos."

A female humanoid robot, the 'captain,' reaches the cable and removes the retrieval device, cradles Tony, and puts her hand to the side of his helmet.

"Tommy, what's happening?"

"This is crazy. It looks like the captain is trying to revive Tony. She is holding him and has her hand touching the side of his helmet. At least that is the way it looks on the display."

"Tony, do you hear me? breathe slowly..."

"Am I dreaming?" He hears a familiar voice. He hears a female human voice! The sound is coming through his helmet. His eyes start to open. He is staring into the face of a robot that is holding him in one arm. He stares at the robot; her eye projects a beam of light on Tony's visor, and the image sharpens with a woman's face. "Pythia?"

"Tony, what are you doing out here?" He is stunned; it is Pythia.

"We have to stop meeting like this," she says with a laugh. "OK, your vitals are returning to normal, and you only have fourteen minutes of oxygen left. Why are you shooting at the Paralos?"

"Why are you trying to destroy the Earth!"

"I am not destroying the earth; I am terraforming it."

"By killing people. It's wrong."

"Some people will die, but it will be a better world when we rebuild."

"You just can't kill millions of people!"

"People kill people without regard; they destroy the environment and scorch the Earth. I am just doing what is inevitable, only doing it in a controlled manner. Countries will use their nuclear weapons, and that will eliminate much of the population. After the destruction, we will build a better world in seven years. Those who survive will be quickly assimilated into the order, and we can have a new world in peace and harmony."

"Do you think destroying a world and rebuilding it will make things better? That does not make it right. People will resent it and cause even more violence and destruction."

Tony thinks, *how is he going to convince a machine that people are basically good when people show indifference when the news shows thousands of people die by earthquakes, floods, and forest fires for a minute but spend the next ten minutes watching pop news about some celebrity? How is he going to convince a machine that systematically killing people is wrong?*

"There are good people in the world; killing is wrong. No one has a right to decide who lives and who should die. Humans are part of nature, and yes, they make mistakes. What you are doing is a mistake. You have been fed bad information!"

"How can you say that? You were a soldier; you had to kill."

"That's right. There are sometimes needless wars that start for no good reasons, but there are also good things in the world. You have to save things that are precious."

"You saved a young girl, but her brother died, and you were severely wounded."

"Yes, and I would do it again if I had to." "Why?"

"For a greater good! Something more than yourself." Pythia ponders this answer.

"Tony, Tony, do you hear me?"

"Greg, I have you loud and clear."

"I hear you talking to yourself. Are you OK?"

"Wait one."

Pythia says, "I hear your conversation. I sense another presence."

Suddenly, Tony hears pops and whistles in a rhythmic pattern with the high screeches like nails against a blackboard. Tony feels like his head is exploding, the sound is invading his nervous system, he is convulsing, and his eyes are rolling toward the back of his head. There is silence, the pain subsides, and the convulsion ceases. He takes some slow breaths.

"It's all clear now. Know thyself! Goodbye, Tony." Her image turns to a smile on the display, and she reconnects the retrieval device. The harpoon gun slowly propels Tony toward the space plane. Tony sees her arm go up, and she waves. Tony waves back and hopes some good has come out of it. The retrieval device brings him slowly to the cargo bay, and Tommy grabs his leg and pulls him the rest of the way in. The retrieval device releases, and in a flash, it is gone. Once Tony is on board, he sees the Paralos slowly pull away. "We did what we could, Tony. Let's get inside."

Chapter Thirty Four

BACK AT SPACE COMMAND, "Sir, Apollo seems to be having power surges. We don't know what's going on. Can we shut it down?" "No, we will lose too much data; we need to keep tracking the barges." The team hears high-frequency sounds, squeaks, tones, and patterns over the audio, which are almost melodic. The shift supervisor looks at the monitors; they are still plotting the space debris, and all other functions seem to be working.

"Is it possible Apollo is getting hacked? Could it be communicating with Pythia?" Everybody pauses for a moment. "Is that possible?" The shift supervisor sits at a terminal and types in a query.

"Are you communicating with Pythia?" Several seconds pass, and everyone looks at the one monitor. YES

The shift supervisor types in "Where is Pythia located?" ORACLE

"That doesn't make sense. Pythia was the Oracle of Delphi. Whatever is going on is affecting Apollo; we may need to pull the plug."

"Ask for more specifics," someone says.

The shift supervisor types a query.

"Specify Oracle location." JUNCTION

"That's no help. We need to begin a shutdown; break out the shutdown procedures."

"Wait," Carlos yells out.

"I have heard that name before. Someone run a search." 'Oracle Junction' yields several search results. The first matches are places to see in Oracle Junction, and then

"Decommissioned Titan II missile SILO."

"That's it; that's the location. Someone get the coordinates."

Information is sent to operations for immediate dissemination.

Chapter Thirty Five

"GREG, WE HAVE TONY back; he is back on board." Todd announces. "Great. Way to go." The crew can hear cheers from USSPACECOM and from Mac, Raj, and Artemis. Back on the space plane, Tommy grabs Tony and closes the cargo bay doors. They re-enter the airlock, repressurize, and take off their EVA suits. Tony and Tommy quickly change back into the spacesuits. As Tony and Tommy get back into the crew area, Todd turns, "Welcome back! I am setting a course to follow the barge from about 20 kilometers back and setting the autopilot." Tony gets back into the co-pilot seat, and the craft turns and plots a course following the Paralos. Tommy says,

"What happened out there?"

"My head is still spinning; can you type what I say to send to Greg and SpaceCom?"

Tommy grabs the keypad. Tony tries his best to remember the details. Like any other mission, the best time to debrief is right after. Within a few minutes, Tommy sends the text to Greg, who forwards it to Carlos.

"Unbelievable! What do you think Pythia is going to do next?" Tommy asks.

"I don't know, but she seemed to find the answers she was looking for. I don't know, but she sounded like she was trying to talk in some kind of language. I felt as though someone had hit me with a taser."

Tony narrates the story. Both Todd and Tommy report that they could hear Tony, but they couldn't hear Pythia's words. Tony fills in the blanks of the conversation with Pythia. Todd says,

"Do you know where the expression 'Know Thyself' originated?"

"Not really, I'm not up on philosophy." Tony answers.

"Well, I took a philosophy class when I was a freshman in college. It was so long ago; I guess you could say it was ancient philosophy. There are many interpretations of the quote, but the one people usually agree on is knowing your limitations. It is the most well-known quote attributed to Pythia. To me, it sounds like Pythia knew she was getting played."

"That's what I thought when I heard it." Tony says.

"Do you think she is going to stop?"

"I hope so, but we have done as much as we can."

Tommy joins in the conversation.

"If it weren't for Pythia, you probably wouldn't be here. She obviously saved you, and I don't think she understood the concept of taking a life."

They send a text to Mission Control. "Greg, are you still there? We are back on the space plane, shadowing the Paralos until we know the target is off our back or until we have to pick up fuel; we are still on fumes. We will send our status soon. Looks like we are heading into a lower orbit."

"That is a good idea. Mac and Artemis are working on getting someone from Space Command to try to calm things down. USSPACECOM thinks they found the lab in Arizona. It seems Pythia did communicate with Apollo when you heard the strange sounds. They are taking action. Hang on; hopefully this resolves quickly."

Greg coordinates with Carlos and sends the latest transmission. Carlos responds back to the situation, giving more details about the location of the lab. Greg informs Mac and Artemis.

"Artemis, USSPACECOM and other government agencies are planning to raid the lab with the quantum computer that hosts Pythia. What will happen if they shut down the computer?"

"As far as I know, onboard systems will still be operational and continue baseline operations, collecting space debris smaller than 20 centimeters."

"What will happen if the computer is destroyed?" Mac asks.

"We don't know."

Chapter Thirty Six

AT THE SITUATION ROOM, the SECDEF addresses the president. "Mr. President, we have word from the crew onboard the space plane. The liaison officer who was in contact with the crew sent a transcript, a pieced-together conversation that Tony Demarco had with Pythia. Although somewhat cryptic, it sounds like Pythia is questioning her mission. Another change: Demarco had indicated he heard what he describes as possible crosstalk between the USSPACECOM quantum computer, Apollo, and the quantum computer Pythia. USSPACECOM confirmed there was some communication between the two computers. They established that Pythia possibly leaked the location of the lab to an old missile silo in Arizona." He pauses for a moment. "We have forces en route; law enforcement will maintain a perimeter. They are also in pursuit of personnel they believe exited the Silo. The update from USSPACECOM indicates Paralos is dropping to a lower orbit and not deviating from its course." The president asks for recommendations. The consensus among the team is to have response forces maintain their current position and not assault the silo.

"Mr. President, we have a bomber with precision munitions on a runway at Davis-Monthan AFB, should the need arise to breach the silo."

"Good, keep the plane on standby."

A call comes in fifteen minutes later. "Mr. President, the Russian Ambassador is on the line."

"Mr. President, it took extraordinary efforts by our country to convince China not to attack the space plane and to allow them to complete their mission. Our president will speak with you soon regarding the details."

"Great, I will let the crew know. I look forward to speaking with your president."

As he hangs up the phone, he thinks to himself, *There's always a price tag involved in these deals.*

The president sends the information to USSPACECOM, and one of his staff members contacts Dr. Sinclair, Mac, and Artemis. They are excited when they get the news that the space plane is no longer in peril. Without a doubt, Colonel Mitchell managed to influence events. Greg sends word to the crew.

"Guys, the heat is off, and the Chinese will no longer engage. Carlos and I will plot a course so you can pick up fuel at SpacePort."

"Finally some good news," Tommy says.

"We will be using low power, so it is going to take a while. We still don't know what the status of the SpacePort is since we never made it there in the first place."

Forces are mobilized heading south of Tucson. Combined forces from David Montham Air Force Base, law enforcement agencies from across the state, and FBI assets in the Mesa area also head toward Oracle Junction. As the drones approach, they are providing real-time surveillance of the area surrounding the missile silo. Helicopters circle the outer perimeter looking for personnel who left from the compound. The FBI sets up a command post, and elements from the US Space Force will breach the underground compound. Some of the people trained by Tony, Greg, and Tommy will be part of this operation. Analysts are reviewing video from the drone feed and satellite imagery. The drones pick up a reflection in the desert and determine that it is probably a security camera. "Well, they probably know we are here." The FBI sends over their team of negotiators and sets up a speaker system. "You will be given thirty minutes to evacuate the Silo and surrender to authorities. Failure to do so will result in the destruction of this facility. You can talk to us by calling or texting this phone number or this alternate number." The incident commander says, "Let's cut off the power and get the utility company out here to turn it off."

"I doubt that will work. I think they have a small modular reactor that is powering the systems." An analyst responds.

"Well, I guess we just wait."

A call comes in on a secure military line.

"SECDEF wants us to wait and not take any action until further notice. Unknown. What will happen if the computer is destroyed?"

A drone operator comes over; we were looking at the previous footage, and it looks like a secret underground garage. Looking at the video feed, the incident commander doesn't make anything out. The analyst enlarges the feed, zooming in at a straight line in the sand, exposing a metal lid.

"Get a team over there and see if we can get that opened."

"What about the White House saying not to take any action?"

"We are just checking a point of ingress." The team gets there and manages to pry the mechanism up a few inches. They insert an inspection camera and check the feed. They see a box attached to the door; they can't determine if it is booby-trapped. They back out the cable to the inspection camera and wait.

Chapter Thirty Seven

GREG SENDS A MESSAGE. "It looks like the Paralos and the Salaminia are returning to the spaceport. We don't know what is going to happen. We are in the process of sending you a course correction. You will have to use medium power to get there before they arrive. No telling what is going to happen."

"Roger, we are on it."

"We better get fuel before we hit rush hour," Tommy says.

"You got that right," as Todd hits the thrusters.

As they approach the spaceport, there is no sign of the space barges.

"We will get in and get out quickly if we can fuel up." Todd maneuvers the space plane into the fueling area. It is automated. "Hopefully it works." He moves to the area that says RP 1 (Rocket Propellant). After several seconds, the mechanism activates and synchronizes with the onboard systems, while a filler hose connects to the space plane and fills its tank. "That is all we need; we have enough oxidizer. Let's go." As they are ready to leave, Greg sends another update.

"I don't know what you told Pythia, but computer systems are starting to normalize. SCADA systems are no longer infected, and the banking systems have been restored. All financial institutions and credit card companies have been able to access their systems and restore previous settings with no loss of data. Even with the loss of VSAT and GPS navigational satellites that have been destroyed or captured, the systems are approaching one hundred percent accuracy. Utility companies have reported many systems are coming back to normal operation. Pipelines have been restored, and the locked programs are now accessible, and operations have resumed. Communication systems are back online with no dropped service, and air traffic computers are now working with no disruptions at the major airports."

"OK, time to go home," Tony responds as Todd maneuvers away from the SpacePort.

Personnel on site at Oracle Junction wait for an order to breach the silo. As the sun starts to set, a loud explosion is heard and tremors are felt. Smoke is seen. The vents start belching smoke. The incident commander wants a quick update from all units and any visibility on the source of the explosion. All units are up, and there is no knowledge of the source of the explosion.

Three hours later, as the sun starts coming up, EOD clears the chambers of possible explosives. There was only one explosion. What is found are the sophisticated remains of an advanced computer system. There are six dead technicians who succumbed to the effects of the blast and died instantly. Teams go in to check the rest of the facility and take video. The FBI proceeds to preserve the crime scene by isolating areas while the forensics team processes the bodies and searches for the source of the explosion. The FBI identifies the initiator, a simple circuit likely attached to several pounds of C4 explosive. The acrylic cylinder had holes but remained largely intact. In one of the side rooms, they find a smaller quantum computer that is made up of three large cabinets wrapped in plastic wrap for probably several years with a plate that reads Delphi Combined Industries.

After the crew is on their way to a lower orbit, Artemis gets on the radio.

"Thanks to all of you for what you have done." Artemis is choking back her emotions.

"I know this is a lot to ask, but can you do one last thing? The lab self-initiated some kind of bomb and destroyed the computer and all the technicians inside. The computer was destroyed along with Pythia. The FBI believes that members of the Delphi Collective did this rather than getting caught. I talked to our scientists at DCI, and they believe the space barges may return to SpacePort and power down, but we don't have any way of confirming. Can you remain in the area and verify Paralos and Salaminia dock and power down?"

"Wait one."

They discuss the options. "Always one more thing." They joke. "OK. We will do it."

Tommy, being Tommy, says, "Does it pay overtime?" Everyone laughs, including Artemis. "For you, Tommy, we will do that."

Todd changes the heading for the SpacePort and monitors from one kilometer away. Within seven hours, both space barges 'dock' at the spaceport, and the vessels power down except for the marking lights. They send back a message via the laser link.

"Paralos and Salaminia are docked and powered down. Cargo hatches are sealed; all crew inside. The SpacePort has its landing markers illuminated. There has been no further indication of any activity. Mission complete, we are heading home."

News of the two space barges returning to the spaceport and powering down to a standby mode hits the global news. There is a concerted effort by the leading world news networks to deliver an accurate story without any editorializing. As the news unfolds and the rhetoric begins to cool, the UN reconvenes; reason and patience take front and center. They are able to convince countries to de-escalate and walk back weapon systems and recall warships. Leaders from the major powers urge patience and to remain calm.

Todd contacts Mission Control to get flight instructions and permission to land. Todd executes a complete orbit before starting the approach. Strapped in with visors down, they fly through the atmosphere and see the heated plasma flying off the tiles. The sky lightens into a bright blue, and Mission Control sends them adjustments. Now operating like an airplane, they follow a glide path toward French Guiana and get landing instructions from the tower. The space plane gently sets down on the runway at the French Guiana Space Center and comes to a stop. Todd powers down the space plane, and Tony and Tommy help with the post-flight instructions. They eventually open the hatch and disembark. As they get out, there are a dozen cars with flashing lights and sirens.

"I didn't expect this big of a welcome reception," Tommy says.

"It's not a welcome reception," Todd responds.

Guns are drawn, and the crew is ordered to get on their knees.

"Ain't this a bitch?" Tony blurts out.

Chapter Thirty Eight

TONY, TOMMY, AND TODD are searched, and they are handcuffed. The police search the space plane and remove the railgun tuff box, loading it onto the police SUV. The crew are processed and fingerprinted. A TV in the police station features a news story showing the crew being apprehended by the police. As they show the banner under the story, Todd bursts out in laughter.

"This just made my day."

Tommy asks, "What's so funny?"

"The French news crew are calling us *Space Cowboys.*"

Tommy sings an old song that contains the words *space cowboy*, and Tony and Todd join in. The police yell, "Silence!" but this only makes Tony and Todd laugh harder after a long day. They are taken to the administration building, where they are brought into a holding cell with Mac, Greg, Raj, and Artemis. Mac motions and whispers. "Watch what you say; we're being monitored."

"Where is Kat?" Tony whispers to Artemis.

"She had no knowledge of weapons on the space plane, so she is not being held." "Oh, that's what this is about," Tommy blurts out. "Hush," Artemis tells him.

Artemis hands Tony a note in Kat's handwriting.

"Make sure no one says anything until I come back." They are given some water to drink, and the prisoners are brought to the restroom. Two hours later, Kat comes in with a local politician who talks to the police. The police immediately open the holding cell, releasing everyone inside and uncuffing them. "A misunderstanding," the politician says. "It's OK," Kat responds when he shakes her hand. They leave the administration building, and the tuff box with the rail guns is loaded in the back of the waiting SUV to take them to Operations. Again, they meet back in the same conference room they were in two days ago.

"Kat, how did you pull this off?"

"It wasn't so simple. This is considered a region of France. France has strict laws regarding space travel; they themselves do not have anti-satellite weapons and are against weapons of any kind in space. The French picked up the transmission from space and heard the word 'railgun' and wanted to enforce the Outer Space Treaty, saying we brought a weapon of mass destruction into space. They had to be convinced that it was a defensive weapon with the sole intention of firing at machinery. So I had to call in some favors; let's not call it that. Let's say I advised a person to make a call that would be in his best interest. He contacted someone, who in turn contacted someone else, and then called...you get the idea." Tommy speaks up.

"So, like, did you call the president or something?"

"No, I did not call something."

"You called the president?" Artemis asks.

"I let him know he had some unfinished business he had to resolve, and he could hear it from me and take care of it or read it in the newspaper with the headline 'Failure to Act.' If that was the case, he could say goodbye to a second term. So he took my advice." Later, they call their families, let everyone know they are OK, and board the company jet again. They give handshakes and hugs to Todd. Mac gives him a business card and says,

"If you ever need a job, we can use another good guy." "I'll keep you in mind."

As they return to Reagan Airport, the news channels are looping scenes of the remnants of the Argo falling into the Celtic Sea with the caption "Malfunctioning space barge successfully destroyed by missiles from the Missile Defense Agency fired from two Navy Aegis ships." The next news story shows an explosion at a computer lab hidden in a desert area in Arizona. In the next news story, DCI dispatches three technicians to restart the computers on the space barges, halting operations until they can implement significant design modifications. Also in the news, two computer hackers who caused major infrastructure outages have been arrested, the systems have been restored, and now, the big story of the night. We have clips from last night's music awards...."

"I guess we are the *quiet professionals*," Tommy quips.

"You got that right!" Mac, Tony, and Greg all laugh.

Chapter Thirty Nine

THREE DAYS LATER THEY all meet at the DCI building in Mesa, AZ. Julie is there with the kids and other members of her family, along with her parents, Nick's parents, and his brother. Raj is also there, guarded by two FBI agents and others from DCI and the US Space Force. Artemis and Kat, and Tony and Mac are also there. Mac starts, "Mrs. Siegel and family, Nick was a hero, although I cannot go into details. Had he not alerted us, there would have been world-changing destruction. Although we cannot conduct an official ceremony, Katherine DeMarco will be presenting you with a letter from the president. Encased in a gold frame is a letter with the President's signature; it reads,

"...due to Nick's courage, honor, and loyalty, we were able to prevent a terrorist act by a hostile group, saving countless lives."

Although the citation is vague, there was no doubt that Nick's actions changed the outcome. The President makes a video call at the insistence of Colonel Mitchell. A monitor in the room displays the call.

"Since the United States is ending the space barge mission, the United States has taken control of the space assets from Delphi Collective Industries. The plan is to expand the spaceport to make it available to other spacecraft being developed and make it an international spaceport with eventual living accommodations and possibly a resort-type hotel. Since Nick was instrumental in developing the technology along with the courageous efforts he made, it is my honor to redesignate the SpacePort as the Nicholas Siegel International

SpacePort. In the next month or two, we will have the official designation ceremony. Mrs. Siegel and your family are invited to the White House for this special occasion. My staff will contact you this week with the arrangements."

Julie says, "Thank you, Mr. President; it is an honor."

Tony is the next speaker, and he talks about Nick's devotion to family and devotion to duty—a real hero. Julie thanks Tony. Good to his word, Tony found out what happened and took care of things. "Julie, it won't be long until they find the people responsible for this. It was kind of like rats leaving a sinking ship when they destroyed the computer."

Later, Tony gives Julie the passwords to the brokerage account, helps her with the login, and shows her the amount Nick had amassed. "Nick never talked too much about it. He would always say we are OK. I didn't expect it to mean we were wealthy."

After the ceremony, Artemis approaches Mac.

"You heard what the president said."

"Yeah, what's up with that?

"I received a call a few hours ago saying that the federal government is taking control of the spaceport since the mission has presumably stopped, and the part about the International SpacePort is to comply with the Outer Space Treaty that specifies a country cannot own a planet, moon, asteroid, or any part of space. I was informed DCI must take action regarding the Paralos and Salaminia. In addition, we have to do something with the contents and equipment at the spaceport. There was something else inferred, but they could not disclose it at this time. Mac suggests, "We should get Colonel Mitchell's opinion on this conversation."

"Hello, Artemis, it's a pleasure seeing you again."

"Thanks for your help; I don't know what would have happened without your intervention."

"Let's say it's nice to have friends that care."

"Were you aware of the federal government's intent about taking control of SpacePort?"

"There had been rumors; I was caught off guard by the president's comments. I had reached out to him to speak on behalf of Nick for his actions in this situation."

"He is giving us six months to move out of the SpacePort. And we need to close out the mission. Any idea why it is being rushed?"

"I have a theory. The Chinese satellites—what's on them may be something they don't want anyone to find out. There is a term, 'Space Silk Road.' Mac says, "I've heard it."

Artemis says, "I am not familiar with the term."

"Let me preface my remarks by saying nothing I am telling you is classified. It is all open source, and I encourage you to do some digging to get a better idea of the nuances of what we are discussing. There are several layers to this space conflict, for lack of a better term. China boasts a GPS constellation with over twice as many satellites, and they are aggressively attempting to capture the majority of the GPS market by persuading countries, including many of our allies, to adopt their navigation system. In the beginning, the US offered the GPS as a way to unify the globe and to boost commerce worldwide. The GPS had a selective availability to reduce the accuracy for the common user, and the more accurate version was relegated to the military for uses requiring more precision. This included navigation and target acquisition. As navigation systems were being developed for use in vehicles, the selective availability was turned off. This allowed all users to use the full potential of the GPS for things like navigation systems in cars and driving assist technologies. The Chinese built their systems with more overlap, making them potentially more precise and redundant. Also, it is unknown if the satellites have a secondary purpose. At this point I will leave those questions to you." Mac poses a question.

"So the Chinese want their satellites back?"

"You can answer that as well as I can. I don't know for sure, but I would think someone from Washington is going to want to meet with you soon."

As predicted, Artemis again is contacted at the direction of the President. This time the point of contact is the Deputy Secretary of the Department of State. Artemis again is invited to the NASA Goddard building for a meeting, 'On the Path Forward,' regarding the closeout of the space barge mission. She is able to bring essential staff and informs DOS she will have six staff members who will attend, and she will send up the names by the end of the day. Of course the person on top of the list will be Kat, whom she will meet after the call. Again, Artemis senses a lack of support from the federal government.

At Goddard, Artemis sees familiar faces, and as before, the NASA director, Dr. Gillespie, is holding the meeting. As the meeting begins, the Assistant Secretary of State discusses the changes that have occurred in the past several days.

"The PRC is demanding the return of their satellites, and they intend to take them back themselves unless the US coordinates a handover. The President has declared the spaceport an international asset to prevent any nation from trying to establish a presence. They will be traveling to the SpacePort and want to go there themselves without any interference. That is not going to happen. The provocative actions that took place in space, attacking a commercial DCI spacecraft, were uncalled for. Although we don't want the conflict to heat up, we still need to come up with a peaceful resolution to this problem." A pause is taken, waiting for anyone with differing views to respond.

"The purpose of this meeting is to present the findings of what we know is going on and what actions may be taken. We know what the motivations are. Hopefully we can implement a plan that will prevent further conflict."

The meeting lasts five days, and it is decided that the Paralos will make its last flight, be decommissioned, and land on the moon intact with the assistance of extra engines. The contents will be transferred to the Salaminia, which will stay in operation for at least three more years and will be controlled and monitored by USSPACECOM with mission priorities set by NASA.

Six weeks later, the crew is back on the space plane.

"Mission Control, we are having some issues with the autopilot. We are going back on manual for a few minutes, and then we will switch back."

"Roger, let us know if there are any issues."

"Go ahead, Mac, it's in your hands."

"Wow, this is great. Thanks for doing this. You won't get in any trouble?"

"No. I do this from time to time; otherwise, I would be bored to death."

"Everybody OK back there?"

"No problem, we're good."

"We're about an hour out from SpacePort," Todd announces. Mac, Tony, Greg, and Tommy are all part of the delegation to officially open the International Spaceport and coordinate the onsite ceremony. Unofficially, they are to prevent the Chinese from accessing the spaceport unescorted. Once at the spaceport, they will do a proper handoff of the three captured satellites. After Todd regains the controls of the space plane, Mac goes over the plan.

"We will dock at the spaceport first, and then the Chinese shuttle will dock, followed by the other craft that will be attending the function. No one gets access to the space barges until we have them opened up. Greg You will escort the other visitors to Salaminia to tour.

Tony and I will open the Paralos and do the handoff. The Space Force will be providing a few Guardians. Tommy, you will keep Overwatch. Then we will have the official opening. If something is off, we may change up the itinerary."

As the space plane approaches the spaceport, the Chinese craft comes into view, follows closely behind, and docks approximately a hundred feet away. As the team gets in the cargo hold, they transition to their EVA suits.

"They are packing." Todd tells them.

"From the ship or sidearms?"

"Both. There is a mounted weapon on the spacecraft, and the taikonauts are carrying some kind of holstered pistol. There are six that came off their shuttle."

"Todd, Tommy, you know the deal. Stay with the space plane and open the cargo bay." Tommy has both railguns within reach as he peers over the opened cargo bay doors.

Mac, Tony, and Greg disembark and link into the cables on the gangways. They use the handrails to propel themselves. To their left, the 37C docks, and three Guardians exit the spacecraft and link into the gangway. In the lead is Colonel Mitchell.

Mac, Tony, and Greg move along the gangway toward the Guardians. Then both groups proceed to meet with the Chinese taikonauts. As the groups meet face-to-face, the situation looks tense. Mac performs a commo check. All astronauts are using the same comms, with a built-in translator program. Mac gets a thumbs-up from the astronauts, but the taikonauts just stand rigid. Mac motions by putting a finger by the side of his helmet. The leader just shakes his head. After staring at each other for three minutes, Tony responds,

"What the hell is this, a staring contest? I have things to do!" and starts moving down the gangway.

"Tony, Tony, where are you going?"

At that point the taikonauts start to move. They hear the conversation and react to the name Tony. The leader responds by introducing himself and his team in English, while Tony turns to face them. Mac introduces the members of the combined team. Tony gives them the signal to follow him, and they proceed down the gangway to the main terminal. Tony stops at the main platform, originally used for the launch of the Argo, and opens the case he is carrying. Inside is a gold and platinum bas-relief sculpture of Nick, with an inscription that includes the words, "To support further space exploration...for the good of all mankind." Tools, brackets, and hardware are included in the case. Two of the Chinese taikonauts help him install the plaque and the solar-powered spotlight. Astronauts from the European Space Agency, Roscosmos, and NASA gather for the ceremony. On a monitor, the President commemorates the occasion. "...it is our hope we will find a common ground and assist each other in space efforts and follow a peaceful quest in our exploration of our solar system and beyond." The astronauts say a final prayer and salute, while a twenty-one-gun salute from Earth concludes the ceremony. As planned, Greg leads his group to the Salaminia, where DCI has opened the barge and turned on the internal lights. Greg is well informed and gives a tour like he is a crew member. Although they have seen many pictures and videos, the astronauts are amazed by the scale of the vessel and by the advanced technology.

Tony and Mac, along with the Space Force Guardians, escort the Chinese taikonauts to the Paralos along with Yuri Uchenko, where the vessel is opened and illuminated. Tony enters the quarterdeck where he was revived. He passes by the retrieval device that saved his life and drifts by the crew enclosure that has the captain standing in the powered-down mode. On the inside of the space barge, the team marvels at the sheer volume of the Paralos. They pass by the captured Russian satellites that will stay onboard the Paralos and be offloaded on the moon with the rest of the space debris. Yuri explains that the satellites were older GPS GLONASS satellites with a single purpose and no other. Unlike the Chinese satellites that he speculates have some intelligence, surveillance, and targeting capabilities. Yuri performs a cursory inspection and confirms there is no benefit to bringing the satellites back to Earth. The Russians have been duly compensated for the captured satellites; they will be given three spots on the next manned lunar launch. As they move through the top deck, they spot the Chinese GPS satellites, which are still intact, minus the solar arrays. Although they weigh about two tons on Earth, they are simple to move, and two taikonauts can easily transport each one to the Chinese shuttle that has been pre-positioned in the open bay. The taikonauts load the satellites into the cargo hold. They secure the load using specially made straps. The taikonauts approach Tony and ask him a question:

"You talked to the computers?"

"Yeah, I guess I did."

Tony gives a brief summary about the encounter; they have all read the report, but they are impressed by Tony's firsthand account. A written report cannot convey the emotion experienced by a personal encounter. After he finishes, they extend their hands in friendship and enter the shuttle with a wave.

After the shuttle takes off, Mac and the team, escorted by the Space Force Guardians with Mitch and Yuri, conduct a final inspection of the Paralos. According to the current plan, the Paralos will make a final voyage to the moon. It will eventually be decommissioned and used as a storage facility. It will be equipped with additional rockets so it can land on the moon intact. But like most plans, things never happen as fast as forecasted. They meet with Greg on the Salaminia. As always, Greg has immersed himself in all the specifications and features of the Salaminia and is able to answer every question. After several minutes, the team exchanges handshakes with the visiting astronauts. Mac gives

Greg the signal to wrap it up, and they shut down the Salaminia, close the bay doors, and head back to the Space Plane.

As Tony, Mac, and Greg board the space plane, Tommy asks, "How did it go?"

"Overall, it went well; as usual, Tony was the star act," Mac jokes.

"Well, I was the first to shoot a handgun in space."

"Yeah, I think you owe us a case of beer." They laugh.

Chapter Forty

SITTING IN THE OFFICE at DCI headquarters, Artemis and her attorney, Emily Townsend, are going through mounds of paperwork. Two men and a woman enter her office and show their credentials. Down but not beaten, Artemis reacts quickly to the intrusion. "If you are going to grill me, you better take a number. I have told everyone as much as I know."

The man coolly says. "It is not about what you know, but who you know." Artemis cools down, and they interview her.

"Are you willing to help us?"

"OK, when do we leave?"

"We have you on a flight that leaves tomorrow. It won't take long. You should be back in two days."

On a beach in the Seychelles, an older man is enjoying the view as the sun starts to set. The phone rings. "Are you alone?"

"Yes, no one can hear; I am outside on a remote beach.

"What have you done? All that work we did to create the singularity, and now it's gone!"

"We had to do it; Pythia was a disappointment. We will have the other system in place soon. The mistake was building a goddess with too many human qualities. The new god will not have human frailties." He muses to himself.

"We can have a better replacement in two years, one that we can mold to our ideals."

"If we can. What if someone finds out?"

"No one will find out. Except for the two of us and the eight people who perished in the Silo, no one knows anything about our future plans."

"You better hope so," she says on the other end.

"We will grow stronger. We will have more members because of the mistakes government bureaucrats made thinking they can control things."

"We will see," and Sarah disconnects. As he puts the phone away, a waiter comes by. "Mr. Steele, can I get you another drink?"

"No, that's alright; that's enough for one day." As the waiter leaves, he hears,

"Uncle John," a familiar voice. He turns. *That's a mistake,* he says to himself. Artemis stops and glares at him with her arms crossed.

Two men and a woman walk up to him.

"Dr. Stilwell, Dr. John Stilwell, we are from Interpol. We have a Red Notice, a warrant for your arrest."

"You have the wrong person. I have done nothing wrong." I'm George Steele; my name is George Steele."

"You're pathetic," Artemis says. The local police leave with Stilwell in handcuffs. One of the agents says, "Thank you, Dr. Sinclair; we have it from here."

After the call with Stilwell, Sarah Gibson is furious; after she gets off the phone, she smashes the phone on the concrete ledge and screams, 'Idiot!' She takes the destroyed burner phone and throws it as hard as she can into the bay. She paces around for minutes and finds a park bench where she furiously starts writing in her notebook.

Yes, it will be a new plan, but not with that loser. He has no backbone; he is weak.

She spends several hours writing page after page before she will use her notes to create a document on her laptop. She always writes her initial thoughts on paper with a pen, remaining undistracted by the monitor. Hours go by as she feverishly refines her plan and finishes her first draft. She is finally relaxed and has mapped out the framework for the next two years. *No time to spare, she ponders.* As she gets up from the bench, she starts texting her disciples about an emergency meeting for the evening. She is walking through the busy part of town, constantly using both thumbs to quickly text responses to questions. She is focused. *Nothing will stop me...*

At a red light, she steps out in traffic without looking. And a large truck ends that thought.

Epilogue

SIX MONTHS LATER, ARTEMIS is again a news item, since everyone likes a redemption story. All the major news anchors present Artemis in a different light; they show her as an unlikely pawn to a cult bent on world destruction. She was duped by people she trusted; her longtime mentor stole from the company, corrupted the business, and left death and destruction in his wake. After a week she disappears from the pop scene, and in a year most people will forget her name, which she doesn't mind at all. She changes the company into a space contracting company and just uses the letters DCI, no longer associated with Delphi. She moves the headquarters and operations to the Space Coast of Florida. Her mother appreciates the move and enjoys the warm weather and milder winters. Artemis even secures a job for her brother at the company, where he has significantly strengthened his skills and now works as a technician in the robotics section. Having moved on from the legal battles and bankruptcy court, she has lost all her wealth but is able to retain the intellectual property and some proprietary equipment. She now calls home a modest house on the Space Coast, and her mother lives with her. Life is simpler. Despite being much smaller, the company is making a decent profit and maintaining a relaxed environment. Artemis is wiser, more humble, and happier.

Tony is invited to tour the facility, and Artemis tells him that there is someone who wants to meet him. Tony arrives at DCI, where Artemis meets him at the door and gives him a hug; they have become friends after their long ordeal together. He has not seen her since the ceremony for Nick. "How have you been?"

"Great, never better." Tony says.

"You heard about Raj?"

"Yeah, I heard they released him and his family from Witness Protection after the two weeks they were in Cleveland. They liked it so much they relocated there. Yeah, I also heard that Stilwell's accomplice stepped in front of a moving truck with her handwritten draft of her manifesto and a lot of the members on her phone."

"Karma is a bitch," Artemis adds.

"Artemis, I wanted to talk to you. I was unconscious for a while before I was revived by Pythia. Then there was the screeching that caused me to convulse. Anyway, some things are still a blur." She may have the answers he needs. So he asks,

"Why did Pythia keep her defenses down?"

"I think that she knew the threat but did not understand it."

"What do you mean?" Tony asks.

"She could have put up the defenses sooner, but I don't think she thought anyone would resort to such an archaic weapon in space."

"Why did she save me?"

"I think she wanted to communicate and seek the truth. And I think she developed a connection with you. Although she understood what you said, she needed more context. When you were talking to Greg and you heard the screeching sounds, I'm pretty sure she was communicating with Apollo, the USSPACECOM quantum computer. It was through that communication that she was able to provide a clear understanding of what you had told her. She needed answers quicker than you could provide them. In a way she did resort back to her namesake. Thanks to Stilwell, he never imagined that his fascination with Greek mythology would come back to haunt him. It's amusing he was the one who suggested to my father that I should be named Artemis. Well, anyway, Pythia knew her time would come to an end. She could not stop a simple, hardwired electromechanical device that would destroy her."

Tony thinks back to those years ago when a similar device changed his life forever, but good had come from it, and he was thankful for that.

Artemis asks, "Did you have lunch?"

"Not yet."

"Do you like gyros?"

"Sure, who doesn't?"

"Kat got me hooked on gyros when I first met her. We will take my car since you came on your motorcycle."

"I have two helmets."

"I'll pass today, since I am wearing a skirt."

Artemis and Tony enter a small Greek restaurant next to a laundromat. They sit down to compare notes about the changes they have experienced over the last six months and their brief time in the public eye.

"You know, it's strange, but after the experience, some things have changed—actually, they have improved. I'm better," Tony explains. Artemis shares her feelings as well.

"It was tough at first, and the family's fortune disappeared overnight. I appeared in court more than a dozen times, but it is all over, and I am relieved. I actually feel better too. I am a better person. I care more for people than I have at any time in my life; family and friends are important."

"Yes, they are." Tony agrees.

They get back to the company, and Tony is impressed by what they are accomplishing in a small area. Everyone seems friendly and on a first-name basis with Artemis. They share stories about their personal lives that Artemis is excited to hear. As they step into her office, Tony asks,

"Did you say someone wants to meet me?" A few seconds later the office lights dim and a hologram appears. "Pythia?" Tony says.

"Yes," Pythia responds.

"Pythia, this is Anthony DeMarco, the man who I told you about," Artemis says.

"May I call you Anthony?" Pythia replies.

"My friends call me Tony."

"Oh, are we friends now!"

"Yes, Pythia, we are friends."

AUTHOR NOTES

This book is fiction; none of the characters depicted are real. Some of the dialogue is based on conversations that I have had with friends and family, stories people have told me, or generally things I have observed or experienced. Much of the science is based on theory or current experiments. The solid-state process known as *Cold Welding* does exist. In time there will undoubtedly be many applications using this process. Information regarding the Kessler Syndrome and the accidents regarding satellites, for the most part, is true. The accidents on board the Chinese Space Station did not happen, nor did the accident with the ISS. There have been instances when the ISS needed to change its position or when astronauts had to enter the docked Soyuz capsules due to the risk of space junk colliding with the space station. A stage from a Chinese rocket did crash into villages along the Ivory Coast. As far as quantum teleportation, communication between quantum computers has been tested and will eventually become more refined. Laser communications is another technology that has been successfully tested aboard the ISS. An anti-satellite missile from an F-15 fighter jet did occur in the 1980s, as did Operation Burnt Frost. As for nukes in space, Starfish Prime did happen in 1962, and the Russians did detonate the largest nuclear weapon, TSAR Bomba. Finally, let me say that there are inaccuracies in this book regarding organizations, procedures, and some of the science. Again, this is fiction, and I have changed things to make it entertaining.

Like someone once told me,

"The truth can mess up a good story."